COPYRIGHT

Johnnie Copyright © 2015 Cardeno C.
ISBN: 978-1-942184-24-9
Print ISBN: 978-1-942184-35-5

Issued by: The Romance Authors, LLC, March, 2015
http://www.theromanceauthors.com

Editor: Jae Ashley
Interior Book Design: Kelly Shorten
Cover Art: Arianne Elliott

DEDICATION

To Toni Hanks: Thank you for your support and for naming the Berk pride. And most especially, thank you for honouring Johnnie with your grandfather's name.

CHAPTER 1

OVER a decade had passed since he'd last experienced the overly-full feeling, so Hugh Langley didn't immediately identify the cause. He continued thrusting, enjoying the warm bodies, hungry grunts, and musky scents of the lion shifters around him, when suddenly, the pressure in his head and chest swelled and nearly knocked him unconscious. That was when he realized what was happening.

"Where's the Siphon?" he asked breathlessly as he pushed himself to a kneeling position and darted his gaze around his large bedroom. This was worse, so much worse than it'd ever been. He could barely breathe, barely think, barely move. "The Siphon?" he gasped.

"Hugh?" said Mara Terrence, the shifter who'd been writhing beneath him. "What's wrong?"

"Premier?" Dennis Jones untangled himself from Percy Milroy and both men approached him. "What's... Oh, fuck! Mara, hold onto him before he falls."

"What's wrong with him?" Mara cried as she balanced Hugh's considerable weight and lowered him to the floor.

"What's going on?" Lorena Mansfield said as she rushed out of the bathroom, where she'd been cleaning up before heading home to make dinner for the dozen cubs living in her house.

"The Siphon," Hugh bit out as he clutched both sides of his head. "Find the Siphon."

"He isn't in here."

"The Siphon can't be far from the Premier," Percy pointed out. "Look in his room!"

Within seconds, the door connecting Hugh's bedroom to the Siphon's slammed open.

"Oh shit!" Dennis screamed. "I need help! Mara, Lorena, Percy, someone get in here. Hurry! Before he hurts our Premier."

"What... Dennis! Hugh's seizing," Percy said. He cupped Hugh's cheeks with his clammy, trembling hands and begged. "Hugh. Premier. Please don't die. We need you. Please don't die."

One moment, Hugh had no control over his twitching limbs and useless lungs, and the next, he felt an opening into the tunnel that connected him to the Siphon. With the last of his energy, he shoved his power through it, and finally, blessedly, relieved the disabling pressure tearing him apart from within.

"Hugh?" Percy said, his voice trembling. "Can you see me?"

The darkness cleared from Hugh's vision and he blinked as he sucked in air.

Percy was crouched over him, his normally tan skin, milky white and his brown eyes huge. "Premier?"

"I'm okay." Hugh coughed and sat up. He patted Percy's shoulder, his black hands wildly contrasting with Percy's unusually pale body. "Everything's fine."

"Hugh?" Mara, Lorena, and Dennis rushed over and dropped to their knees beside him.

A rare Premier lion, Hugh's power and energy put his pride members at peace and made them strong and confident, which allowed for success in all facets of their lives. The pride adored and revered him, so the sight of him so near death left them shaken.

"I'm okay. I pushed my power into the Siphon." Hugh looked around. "Where is he?"

"In his room," Dennis said, his lips curled up in disgust. "How could he do that to you? To our pride?"

"What did he do?" Hugh asked.

"Hanged himself."

A Premier's life spanned centuries, his strength and power growing with every cycle of the sun until, eventually, he could no longer contain the force, leading to a painful death for him and devastation to the pride. But a Siphon siphoned off a Premier's energy. Though he couldn't use it himself, the Siphon provided storage for the power while keeping it available for the Premier's use. A Siphoned Premier was nearly indestructible. *Nearly* because the death of the Siphon would eliminate the energy storage source, leaving the Premier overrun with power until he imploded.

"Don't worry. We cut him down and used the rope to secure his wrists and ankles." Mara glared at the connecting doorway. "He won't be able to hurt you now."

Hugh had been leading the Berk pride for over seventy years when his steadily increasing power had become too large to contain within his own body. Under his guidance and leadership, the Berk pride and its lions had blossomed. A decade earlier, the small, weak Westgate pride had offered him a Siphon who had just come of age in exchange for taking them all into his prosperous Premier Pride. Hugh's agreement had saved the Westgate lions from near certain death.

"Hanged himself?" Hugh repeated in surprise. "Why would he do that?"

The blank stares around him indicated that nobody had considered the question let alone determined the answer. Physically drained and more than a little shaken by how close he had come to death and how vulnerable he had been in front of his lions, Hugh needed to regroup and then investigate the situation with the Siphon so he could make sure it never happened again.

"You said he's secure now?"

"Yes."

Not wanting anybody to view him as weak, Hugh determinedly climbed to his feet and straightened his broad shoulders. Like all Premiers, his skin, hair, and eyes were black in both human and lion forms. And because his body grew along with his power as he aged, at over a century old, he was seven feet tall and weighed three hundred pounds. That size helped him appear stronger and more in control than he felt at that moment.

"I'll get to the bottom of it," he said firmly, making sure his tone allowed for no argument. He walked to his open bedroom door, knowing his pride members would follow him, and said, "We're done here for the night."

All four lions said their goodnights and traipsed out of the house without a backward glance. He sighed, relieved his loss of control hadn't made them doubt his abilities. Unfortunately, the same couldn't be said for his own thoughts.

He had never come that close to dying, not even before he'd had a Siphon. The upside to the incident was indisputable proof of how much his power had grown over the past decade. The downside, however, was how incredibly dependent he was on the Siphon. Exhausted, Hugh returned to his bedroom and collapsed on the mattress, not bothering to pull back the quilt. He would sleep, rejuvenate his body and his mind, and deal with the Siphon when he could think clearly.

Hugh woke up in a pitch-black room. He rolled to his side and squinted toward the huge picture window. By midmorning, light inevitably seeped in from around the corners of the rich silk drapes, the sun-blocking liner unable to keep the rays completely at bay. Not an ounce of light came through, so it was either late Friday night or early Saturday morning.

Though he had healed from the physical effects of the Siphon's action, his worry hadn't abated. Whatever caused the lapse in judgment had to be addressed quickly and firmly. Needing to regain his emotional footing before dealing with the unexpected and unwelcome situation, Hugh headed toward the bathroom.

Once he was clean, dressed, and feeling more like himself, he marched into the adjoining room, flipped on the light switch, and said, "You need to explain yourself."

Curled into a ball on the bed with his ankles and wrists bound together, the Siphon remained silent and still. Hugh would have thought he was dead but for the fact that his death would have meant Hugh's own immediate demise.

When Hugh had taken in the starving Westgate lions and saved them from their fire-ravaged land, they had gained resources, homes, food, and a Premier. With a great deal of work and time on Hugh's part, those lions had integrated with the Berk lions and they now made a cohesive pride that was even more successful than it had been before the merger. But the Siphon had almost destroyed all of that the previous night.

"Wake up," Hugh said.

With a resigned sigh, the Siphon moved, seemingly trying to sit up. The bindings prevented him from succeeding.

"I'll untie you." Hugh was a foot taller and twice the Siphon's weight, so releasing him wasn't a risk. He stepped over, took the rope in both hands and tugged, snapping it with no effort. The display of strength eased the part of him still worried about an ongoing impact from his near-death experience. "Can you sit up?" he asked when he noticed the Siphon still having trouble.

"Yes," the Siphon croaked and shakily rose to a sitting position. "Are we going somewhere?" He rubbed his trembling hand over his neck and began standing. "I'll get my shoes."

"No." Hugh grasped the Siphon's shoulder and held him in place. "I came here to talk to you."

"You want to talk to me?" He blinked in confusion.

"Yes. We need to talk about what you tried to do to our pride." Though based on that hoarse voice, Hugh doubted the Siphon could do much talking. "You need water." He flicked his gaze around the room, which was a silly exercise because there was nothing in the space other than a bed, a nightstand, and a dresser, same as always. The only difference was a hole in the ceiling near the dresser, where Hugh presumed the Siphon had attached the rope. "Let's go downstairs."

"Oh." The Siphon climbed to his feet and then swayed. Hugh waited for him to get his bearings and then slowly walked out of the room. Until he knew what had caused the Siphon's erratic behavior, he needed to be on guard, so he carefully watched him as they made their way to the kitchen.

After getting a bottle of water from the gleaming stainless steel refrigerator, Hugh sat in one of the plush upholstered chairs in front of the magnolia wood kitchen table and waited for the Siphon to get his drink and join him. When the Siphon hadn't spoken by the time Hugh had drained his bottle, he lost his patience and took the reins.

"We can't have a repeat of yesterday. You endangered my pride." Under normal circumstances, Hugh would have killed someone for committing that offense, but the Siphon's death was exactly what he needed to prevent, so he had to come up with a different solution. "Tell me why you hanged yourself."

The Siphon raised the bottle to his mouth, tipped it, and swallowed slowly.

Annoyed at the delay, Hugh considered beating the Siphon into submission, but he had no idea what weakening the Siphon physically would do to his ability to carry Hugh's power. Only one in half a million lions was born a Siphon so there weren't enough of them in the world to know much about them, and Hugh couldn't risk anything that would damage the person who stored his power.

Growling in frustration, he said, "Answer me."

"What do you want to know, Premier?" the Siphon asked tiredly. He fiddled with the label on the bottle.

"I want to know why you tried to kill me and destroy this pride."

"I didn't."

Faster than a normal lion's eyes could track, Hugh grasped the Siphon's throat. "These rope marks say otherwise," he roared, his patience eviscerated. "How dare you lie to your Premier?"

Despite Hugh's show of strength, loud voice, and clear

superiority, the Siphon didn't flinch.

"Answer me." Hugh shook him.

"I did answer." The Siphon's voice was barely audible, both because he spoke quietly and because of the grip Hugh had on him.

"You wrapped a rope around your neck, tied it to the ceiling, and jumped off your dresser," Hugh accused. The Siphon didn't deny the statement, so Hugh continued. "That is an attack on me and this pride." Again, the Siphon didn't speak. Hugh shook him. "Do you deny it?"

For the first time since they had begun talking, the Siphon raised his gaze, laying his uniquely blue eyes on Hugh. "I don't deny hanging myself, but I wasn't attacking anyone."

That answer made no sense.

"I'm over a century old. A Premier my age has too much power to exist without a Siphon." Hugh tossed the Siphon away, making his chair tilt sideways. "You know this. Hell, any cub old enough to climb knows this." He dragged his fingers over his close-cropped hair. "Right?"

After steadying his chair, the Siphon lowered his gaze and nodded.

"And yet you deny that your actions would have left me with no way to contain my energy?"

The Siphon shook his head.

Premiers were rare—one in five thousand lions were born with the black fur and skin marking them as the most powerful lions in existence. But there were a hundred Premiers for every Siphon, making the blue-eyed lions almost unheard of. There was nobody else who could siphon Hugh's power, and on his own, he would implode from its force.

"No more games!" Hugh shouted as he shoved his chair back and jumped to his feet. He planted both hands on the table and loomed over the Siphon. "Berk is a Premier Pride. You could have hurt fourteen hundred full-grown lions and five hundred cubs with your actions. Did you think of that?"

Again, the Siphon shook his head.

"Aren't you grateful?"

His eyebrows drawn together in confusion, the Siphon said, "Grateful for what?"

"For what?" Hugh roared. "Look around." He waved his arm around the room blindly. "You are part of a Premier Pride. We have over four thousand acres of rich land. Our members are well-fed, financially secure, and close-knit. Our homes, businesses, and territory are the envy of most prides. What more do you want?"

"I don't know." The Siphon shrugged and hunched lower in his chair. "To live, I guess."

"You're a Siphon. You can live forever."

Where regular lions lived and aged at the same pace as their human counterparts, Premiers stopped aging when they reached their peak condition and, instead, grew larger and more powerful. And a Siphon who carried a Premier's power aged at the Premier's pace.

"I'm not living." The Siphon licked his lips. "But I'm not dead." Sighing deeply, he whispered, "I want to be."

The conflicting statements made no sense.

"You say you want to live but then say you want to die."
Hugh looked into the Siphon's eyes, hoping to find an answer.
When he couldn't figure it out, he asked, "Why did you hang
yourself?"

"I'm a Siphon. I can't live." The blue-eyed gaze dropped.
"Dying's the only way out."

A foreboding chill ran down Hugh's spine. The Siphon
dying would mean Hugh's own death. He wouldn't allow it.

To carry a Premier's power, a Siphon had to remain
close to him at all times, so Hugh could monitor the Siphon
most of the time. But Hugh slept, showered, fucked. He
couldn't watch the Siphon every second of every day. Bringing
in pride members to guard him wasn't an option because
it would alert them to Hugh's vulnerability, which would
cause turmoil among the pride, and even worse, it would
risk outsiders finding out about it, which would expose a
vulnerability that could easily be exploited.

Eight decades of Hugh's leadership and hard work
had paid off—he hadn't been exaggerating when he'd listed
Berk's attributes to the Siphon. Berk was a Premier Pride,
meaning it was stronger, wealthier, and happier than most
prides. It also meant other lions desperately wanted what
they had, and if they smelled blood, they wouldn't hesitate
to mount an attack. Showing weakness would endanger the
entire pride.

Since age twenty-three, Hugh had dedicated his life to
protecting the Berk pride. If he didn't get to the bottom of the
Siphon's issue, his life and the pride would be in jeopardy. He

wouldn't allow that to happen. But to fix the problem, Hugh first had to understand what it was.

CHAPTER 2

FOR what might have been the first time, Hugh looked at the Siphon. Really looked at him. He was, by all indications, an average lion. Close to six feet tall, about a hundred and sixty pounds, brown hair, golden skin. The only difference was his eyes—Siphon blue instead of the usual brown, hazel, or amber. And they were desolate. Those eyes brimmed with sorrow and exhaustion.

Clearly, Hugh needed a game plan. But he wasn't likely to make progress while the Siphon was in that condition. They both needed sleep, so he said, "It's still early. Let's go back to bed."

He got up and walked out of the room, the Siphon trailing him as usual. When they reached the bedroom and the Siphon walked toward the doorway to his adjoining room, Hugh said, "You'll sleep in here tonight."

The Siphon turned around and looked at him wide-eyed.

"I can't leave you unsupervised," Hugh explained. Though he wasn't a deep sleeper, he still needed to keep the Siphon out of trouble when he wasn't paying attention.

"Oh." The Siphon bit his lip and darted his gaze around

Hugh's spacious room. "There's only one bed. Where should I..."

"I've shared this bed with half a dozen lions at once." Not for sleeping, but screwing used more space than sleeping so it wouldn't be an issue. "There's plenty of room for the two of us."

"Okay." The Siphon flicked his gaze from the bed to Hugh and then looked down at the plush carpet. "But I need to take a shower first."

He'd gotten out of bed, had a drink of water, and come right back to bed. Why did he suddenly need a shower? Hugh began taking a mental inventory of the bathroom, thinking of what the Siphon could use to make another attempt on his life.

"After what happened earlier, I'm sweaty and I don't want to dirty your bed," the Siphon added by way of explanation.

Upon closer observation, Hugh noticed the Siphon's hair was matted down around the edges. Their kind were fastidious about cleanliness, so the assertion likely was true. Regardless, Hugh would keep an eye on him.

"Go ahead," he said.

With a quick dip of his chin, the Siphon turned around and hurried to his room and the attached bathroom. Hugh followed at a more leisurely pace. When he entered the bathroom, the Siphon was standing over the toilet.

"Premier?" he said in surprise, his cheeks coloring as he twisted sideways, hiding his groin.

Public nudity was common for lions. Aside from being naked when they shifted between forms, they had sex whenever the mood struck, regardless of whether other adult lions were present.

"I'm not leaving you unsupervised," Hugh repeated, but the nervousness in the Siphon's blue eyes bothered him enough that he turned around. "There. You have privacy." Not that he understood why the Siphon needed it. "Finish up. The sun will rise soon, and I'll have to get to work."

Protecting the safety and happiness of the Berk pride was Hugh's job, and he took it seriously. Having a strong, visible Premier ensured the prosperity of the pride and sent a message to those outside their territory that attacks wouldn't succeed. His lions needed him to manage disputes, give advice, and oversee the cohesiveness of their extended family. That meant his door was always open. On top of that, Hugh made it a point to visit pride members in their sprawling, communal homes. With nearly two thousand lion shifters in Berk, he was busy from morning, when people rose, to late evening, when they settled into their dens.

After several seconds, he heard liquid hitting the bowl and then a flush. Hugh flipped around to see the Siphon shrugging out of his white oxford shirt with his tan chinos already pooled around his feet. He stepped into the shower, closed the curtain, and then turned on the water.

"Make it fast," Hugh muttered, more because he was uncomfortable standing around waiting on someone than because he was in a particular rush.

After a couple of minutes of silence, save for the running water, Hugh looked around the small room and decided to make good use of his time by checking for things the Siphon could use as weapons. First, he looked under the sink: toilet paper, an extra bottle of shampoo, a box of soap, and a tube of lotion. Nothing potentially fatal. Next, he examined the medicine cabinet: toothpaste, aspirin, a razor, and extra blades. He picked up the box of blades and looked it over, considering whether the Siphon could use them to slice his wrists. He had reached the conclusion that he could and he'd therefore need to use an electric razor instead, when the Siphon spoke from behind him.

"It won't happen."

Hugh flipped around, still holding the box of blades. "What won't happen?"

"Slicing my wrists." The Siphon nudged his chin toward Hugh's hand. "That's what you were thinking, right? That I'd take those blades to my veins and finally find freedom?"

That wasn't actually the terminology Hugh would've used to describe an act that would destroy him and everyone he dedicated his life to protecting.

"That can't happen," the Siphon said, his tone noticeably disappointed.

"You're saying you wouldn't cut yourself?" Hugh asked disbelievingly. If the Siphon was willing to hang himself, admit to Hugh that he wanted to be dead, and describe his demise as freedom, he was likely to try another suicide method.

Completely ignoring Hugh, the Siphon gripped his towel, which was draped around his shoulders like a cape, said, "Excuse me," and then scooted past Hugh into his bedroom.

Having his questions disregarded was unheard of, making Hugh wonder what had brought about the Siphon's sudden personality change. Then he realized that despite the Siphon being his shadow for over a decade, they hadn't talked much. In fact, Hugh was hard-pressed to remember a single conversation they'd had before the previous hour. Instead, he said they were going somewhere, and the Siphon followed silently, always remaining close enough to hold Hugh's power. That aspect of their interaction hadn't changed, so perhaps the Siphon's personality was the same as always. There was no way to know.

Spending his life leading the Berk pride meant having very little downtime, so Hugh was glad that, as the Premier, he lived alone. In addition to eliminating any concerns about favoritism and potential jealousy between lions who would surely vie for his companionship if they believed that to be an option, having his own home gave Hugh space and time to relax without worrying about anybody. But as he stood alone in the bathroom, he realized that had changed. He now had to worry about the Siphon.

He resented losing his only bit of free time, but whatever bothered the Siphon put the entire pride at risk, which was unacceptable. Hugh would make that clear to him. But first, he'd give them both a break for the night. Tomorrow—or later that day—was soon enough for a conversation. Feeling calmer for having a plan, Hugh marched into the Siphon's bedroom.

He stood in front of the dresser, stepping into a pair of inside-out sleep pants. His long-sleeved T-shirt hung on his slender frame, also inside out.

"Your clothes are on the wrong way," Hugh pointed out.

"The seams bother me." The Siphon pulled a sweatshirt over his head.

"You normally dress with your clothes the right way." Otherwise Hugh surely would have noticed before now.

"When I'm awake, it's fine, but I can't sleep with them rubbing against my skin."

Once they were in their respective rooms for the night, Hugh didn't see the Siphon so it was possible he had always slept that way. The sensitive reaction to a part of clothing other people didn't notice struck Hugh as odd. Then again, he slept nude so maybe it was normal. Either way, it didn't matter.

"Are you ready?" he asked.

"I just need my socks." The Siphon opened another drawer and pulled out a thick pair of socks.

"We're indoors," Hugh said. "Isn't that a little overkill?"

"I get cold."

Another odd statement because lions ran hot in both forms. In the winter, Hugh rarely turned on the heater, and in the summer, he kept the air conditioner going nonstop.

For a moment, he wondered if the Siphon was sick.

Illness would explain being cold and achy and maybe the strange behavior too. But carrying a Premier's power meant a Siphon didn't get sick. Except in the face of severe violence or separation from each other, a Premier and Siphon were said to be immortal. There weren't enough Siphons in existence to test that theory, but in over ten years, Hugh couldn't remember the Siphon coughing or sneezing. Then again, he wasn't sure he'd have cared enough about something so mundane to notice it. And unless it related to the Siphon's plan to kill him, Hugh still didn't care.

"Let's go," he said once the Siphon finished putting on his socks.

He flipped around and walked through the adjoining door into his bedroom, the Siphon at his back. He stepped over to the bed, tugged the cover off, and slid underneath the top sheet. After punching his pillow until it was in his preferred shape, he lay down and thought about whether he should restrain the Siphon in some way that'd alert him if he attempted to leave the bed.

Sitting up, he saw the Siphon on the far end of the bed, curled into a ball with the sheet pulled up to his neck. Odd. He was odd. But based on the circles under his eyes and his slumped posture, he was likely to sleep much longer and deeper than Hugh, whose need to be ready to snap to attention and tend to the pride made him a light sleeper. Deciding he could monitor the Siphon sufficiently by sharing a bed, he didn't disturb him to tie rope around his wrist.

Seemingly seconds after he fell asleep, movement woke Hugh. Adrenaline pumping through his body, he shot to a sitting position. He jerked his gaze around the room and confirmed everything was as it should be except that, unlike other nights, he was sharing his bed. He looked to his side and saw the source of the motion: the Siphon, still curled tightly under the sheet, was trembling.

"Are you okay?" Hugh wasn't accustomed to dealing with the Siphon, but a scared pride member was a scared pride member. He was the Premier; he ensured the safety and comfort of the pride. And technically, the Siphon was part of the Berk pride. "Wake up... Uh—" He temporarily tripped over the lack of name to add to the end of that sentence. "Siphon, wake up. You're having a bad dream."

"Not sleeping." The barely audible words were whispered from beneath the sheet.

"You're shaking."

The sheet rustled and then the Siphon popped his head out.

"Why don't I have a name?"

Disconcerted by a question so closely matching his own thoughts, Hugh growled, "You're the Siphon."

"But why don't I have a name?" The Siphon's teeth chattered as he spoke. "Everyone else has a name. You're the

Premier and you have a name. Two names. Hugh Langley. I'm the only one who doesn't have a name."

The Siphon's mind worked in an unusual way, but for Hugh to resolve whatever was plaguing him, he had to understand the stranger in his bed.

"It bothers you?" he asked. "Not having a name?"

"People have names."

"People?" Hugh repeated.

"People. Lions. Everyone has a name."

The Siphon was the Siphon no matter what anyone called him. If a name resolved his issue, the Siphon could have a name.

"What do you want to be called?" Hugh asked.

"I can have a name?" the Siphon said breathlessly, his eyes wide. "Really?"

"It's just a name," Hugh muttered, rolling his shoulders to get rid of the sudden tightness in his muscles.

"What do you think my name should be?"

Hugh opened his mouth to say the name thing was the Siphon's idea so he had no idea what it should be, but even in the dark room, the Siphon's blue eyes sparkled with excitement and Hugh couldn't bring himself to do anything that would take away that hopeful expression.

"What about John?" he said, throwing out the first answer that came to mind. "Do you like that name?"

"John," the Siphon repeated the word slowly, as if he was testing the feeling of it on his tongue. "John is a nice name." He scrunched his eyebrows together in consideration.

"John."

"Or maybe Johnnie," Hugh found himself suggesting as he thought about the air of innocence around the Siphon. "It suits you better."

"Johnnie. Johnnie Langley." The Siphon's face brightened. "I like it."

Langley? The Siphon was going to use Hugh's last name instead of his own mother's?

Adult lions had sex with whoever appealed and was interested at the time; there were no lines, no barriers, and no resulting obligations. The one exception was when a female decided she wanted a cub. In that circumstance, the female carefully picked males whose genes she found appealing. For their part, males were generally honored to be chosen for reproduction so they happily agreed to the advances of any breeding female. To ensure successful procreation, females mated with a handful of potential sires so the ultimate male who fathered a cub wasn't known. Male lions lived with other males while females and cubs lived together alongside other mothers and cubs, with cubs taking their mothers' surnames.

"You don't want to take your mother's name?"

"I don't know who she is."

"How is that possible?"

With a sigh, the Siphon rolled onto his back. "They knew when I was born."

After taking a few moments to consider the comment and what it meant, Hugh said, "Everyone recognized you as a Siphon at birth?"

"Yes." The Siphon nodded. "You know, because of my eyes." He tapped his fingers over one closed eyelid. "They saw blue, knew I was a Siphon, and kept me away from the others." He swallowed loudly. "Or at least that's what I assume happened. It's not like anyone told me, but for as long as I can remember, the pride kept me contained in what was the safest house on our old pride lands."

"They took care of you."

Slowly turning his head toward Hugh, the Siphon pinned him with those blue eyes.

"They wanted to make sure nobody took me and nothing happened to me before I became an adult and could siphon a Premier's power. The pride was dying off and they needed me to attract a Premier. That's what they said."

"So the pride took care of you," Hugh repeated, hoping to remind the Siphon of everything the pride had done for him so he'd stop trying to implement his destructive plan.

"That's how you see it."

Squeezing his fists in frustration, Hugh tried to keep his tone even when he asked, "How do you see it?"

"You want my opinion?" the Siphon asked, his voice squeaking as he arched his eyebrows.

"That's why I asked," Hugh bit out, the circular conversation and inability to get to the root of the problem frustrating him.

"My opinion—" The Siphon rubbed his lips together. "Is that people who care about you, give you a name." His lips curled up slightly at the corners and his eyes fluttered shut.

"Johnnie Langley."

With a contented-sounding sigh, his body relaxed and he fell asleep, effectively ending their conversation and leaving Hugh no closer to an answer about what to do than he'd been before he went to bed.

CHAPTER 3

TEN uneventful days later, Hugh was almost ready to let his guard down. He had kept up with his usual duties to the pride and his visits to their dens, but he had eliminated social interactions after dinner in favor of going back to his house where he could stop pretending there wasn't anything wrong. That time had given him opportunities to talk with the Siphon, and though Hugh still wasn't sure what had made him snap, he hadn't seen any indication of a recurrence. A niggling voice in the back of his head told him the storm was still brewing and the Siphon's soft smiles were nothing more than temporary cloud cover, so he didn't completely relax. But temporary or not, Hugh welcomed any respite from the worry that the Siphon was biding his time for the first opportunity to kill them both.

That reduction in worry allowed Hugh to step into his own room while the Siphon finished bathing. They were getting ready for dinner at one of the dens occupied by females who didn't have cubs. He'd showered while the Siphon waited in his bathroom, and then he'd allowed the Siphon to go to his own quarters and bathe while Hugh supervised. But after looking at himself in the mirror for three minutes with no distractions, he had noticed a pinhead-sized spot on the corner of his shirt, so he dashed into his room to change. When he heard the water turn off through the wall, he headed back to the Siphon.

"Johnnie?" he said as he buttoned up his shirt and walked into the Siphon's bedroom. He was still working on reclassifying the Siphon as Johnnie in his mind, but he made sure to speak the name as often as possible because being called that seemed to have led the Siphon away from the edge of the cliff. "Are you read—"

The sight before Hugh momentarily robbed him of air.

"What is that?" he growled as he dropped his hands from his shirt and stalked over to the Siphon, who was standing on a mat in front of the shower.

"Nothing." The Siphon had been running a towel over his brown hair, but in reaction to Hugh's question, he quickly flicked it over his shoulders in his usual cape-style.

"Don't lie to me." Hugh yanked the towel off him and tossed it aside. "What is this?" He held the Siphon's wrist up in front of his face and shook it. "Answer me!"

Using all his strength, the Siphon tugged his hand free. "It doesn't matter," he said as he wound his arms across his chest and tucked his hands underneath them.

"Those were cut marks. Where'd you get the blades?" Hugh trembled with barely contained fury, the animal inside him clawing to get out. "Give me your hand."

The Siphon shook his head, dropped his chin, and hunched his shoulders.

In a flash, Hugh shifted into his lion form. A normal-sized lion would have barely fit in the Siphon's bathroom; Hugh's beast had no chance. He knocked the Siphon to the ground and stood above him, his thick, muscled body wedged between the wall and the cabinet. Then he raised his head and roared so loudly the walls vibrated.

Eyes wide and nude frame trembling, the Siphon finally did as he was told.

"It doesn't matter anyway," he said as he slid his wrist between their bodies and held it up in front of Hugh's muzzle for inspection. "I told you before, it doesn't work."

The lines on the otherwise smooth skin crisscrossed over one another, some clean, thin, and straight, others thicker and jagged. The combination of adrenaline and being in his animal form kept Hugh from thinking clearly, so he shifted back into his human form, grabbed the Siphon's wrist, and closely examined it. A portion of the cuts were made by a tool, like a razor, but others were claw marks. Lion's claws.

Jerking his gaze up, Hugh stared at the Siphon in shock.

How could he have sliced his veins in lion form? His animal's survival instinct should have prevented it no matter how much his human side wanted it.

"How?" Hugh asked. He straddled the Siphon's hips and clutched his arm. "How could you do this to yourself?" Frustrated at the lack of response, his anger rose and he opened his mouth to demand an answer when he remembered the best way to get cooperation. "Johnnie?" he said, hoping he sounded calm. "Did you make all these marks or did somebody attack you?"

"I'm a Siphon. Who would attack me?"

The answer was nobody. Siphons were so rare that only one in a hundred Premiers was able to obtain one. To ensure the health of their Premier, a pride kept the Siphon secure. And even if another pride and Premier had sought to take over the Berk pride by getting rid of Hugh, they never would have hurt the Siphon because he could be traded to a faraway pride whose Premier was nearing the age when he'd implode without having a Siphon to hold his power. There was virtually no limit to what a Premier Pride would pay in exchange for a Siphon, which made them too valuable to kill.

"You made some of these while you were in your lion form?" Hugh asked, already knowing the answer but needing confirmation of something he previously would have considered impossible.

"It didn't work in my human form."

What Hugh wanted to do was shake the still damp body beneath him until the Siphon talked clearly and gave him complete information. But instead, he climbed to his feet, scooped him off the floor, and walked out of the bathroom.

"What're you doing?"

"We have to talk about what's going on in your head."

"Nothing," the Siphon said.

"Nothing doesn't cause a man to take a razor to his wrist." Or a claw.

"You think of me as a man?" the Siphon blinked up at him, the unusually light eyes focused on his face as if he could ascertain the veracity of Hugh's response by sight.

"You're not a woman, so yes, you're a man."

Gender wasn't relevant to the Siphon's role, and the honest truth was, Hugh hadn't ever thought of him as anything other than a Siphon. But he was a person, just like Hugh and any other member of the pride. Surprised by the simplicity of that revelation, Hugh considered whether that was part of the Siphon's—*Johnnie's*—issue. When they reached his bedroom, he set Johnnie on the sofa and then settled on the upholstered armless chair next to him.

"We cannot continue avoiding this conversation," Hugh said, keeping his tone firm but calm.

"I'm not dressed." Johnnie lifted his feet onto the couch and wrapped his arms round his bent legs.

"If you're cold, there's a throw blanket on the other end of the couch. You can use that."

With a soft nod, Johnnie reached for the blanket. He shook it open, presumably to wrap it around himself, but then he crinkled his nose and reared away from it.

"What's wrong?" Hugh asked.

"It smells bad."

"Oh." Like all lions, Hugh was particular about his environment and meticulous about cleanliness, so he was surprised anything would be dirty.

Rising from his chair, he reached his hand out for the blanket and then lifted it to his nose reflexively as he walked to the laundry basket. The only scents he could identify were those of himself and some pride members, probably from a time they'd fucked in his room and laid the blanket on the wood floor. Those weren't offensive odors, so perhaps the Siphon was sensitive to the particular material. Over the past several days, Hugh had learned that the Siphon had odd sensitivities.

"This should keep you warm." He retrieved a sweater from his closet and brought it to the Siphon. *Johnnie*. That was faster than allowing him to leave the sofa and go to his own room to dress. They had to stop falling prey to distractions and focus on the issue at hand.

"Thank you." Johnnie slipped the sweater over his head and then raised his forearm to his nose and inhaled deeply. "This is better." He closed his eyes, sighed, and with his lips turned up in a small smile, curled into the corner of the couch.

Even his reactions were outside the norm. Shaking off the strangeness, Hugh stayed on target. He'd be calm and rational, they'd get to the root of the issue, and then life could go back to normal.

"Johnnie." He waited for Johnnie to open his eyes and look at him and then said, "We're still ourselves in both forms, but as lions our instincts are sharper and no instinct is stronger than our drive to live. Tell me how you could intentionally injure yourself in lion form."

"For a long time, I couldn't," Johnnie said.

Surprised but pleased that he was getting an answer without the usual requisite prodding, Hugh stayed silent. He leaned forward, rested his forearms on his knees, clasped his hands together, and looked at the Siphon attentively.

"I tried in this form first," he explained, meaning his human form. "But I healed too quickly to be effective."

"You couldn't cut yourself deep enough?" Hugh asked. On the one hand, that reasoning made sense because even in their human form, they were part animal and that part of themselves would do anything possible to stay healthy. On the other hand, the scars on Johnnie's otherwise smooth, creamy skin couldn't have been created by tiny nicks.

"I cut as deep as the razor would go," Johnnie said, his gaze locked with Hugh's. "All the way through the artery."

A chill ran up Hugh's spine in reaction to the hard expression and cool voice.

"You severed your artery and lived?"

Johnnie nodded. "Over and over again." He scrunched his eyebrows together. "That's probably why I have scars. Usually I heal so quickly nothing shows, but after a while, these marks stayed."

"How could you heal from that?" Hugh asked hoarsely.

"I think it's the purring."

Hugh arched his eyebrows in question.

"Before the first drop of blood hit the air, it started. The first time, I didn't understand what it was. The second time, I was surprised it was happening again. The third time, I recognized it. The fourth time, I was ready and tried to stop myself from doing it." Johnnie shook his head. "It didn't work."

"You took a blade to your wrist four times," Hugh said,

registering the information.

"Those were the *first* four. I did it dozens of times after that."

Which was consistent with the marks on Johnnie's wrists, but still shocked and terrified Hugh.

"And you're saying you didn't die because you purred."

Johnnie nodded.

"Like a housecat?" Hugh clarified.

He nodded again.

"We're lions," Hugh pointed out unnecessarily. "We can't purr."

"That's what I thought too." Johnnie shrugged. "Turns out it isn't true. Turns out we can purr. Or at least I can purr."

No part of that story made sense. In the hundred and two years Hugh had been alive, he had never heard of a lion purring. Their bodies weren't made that way. Then again, lions didn't take their own lives, so the entire situation didn't make sense. And Hugh detested things being out of order.

"Show me," he demanded, narrowing his eyes.

"I can't."

"I need to hear this purr."

"Then you'll need to get a knife and cut me open." Johnnie held his wrist out to Hugh. "It's a physical reaction. I can't make it happen just like I couldn't stop it from happening. Cut me," he said as he thrust his arm forward again. "Go ahead and cut me."

Hugh reared back and leaned as far away as he could. "No," he said. "Stop that." He rubbed his palms over his eyes and tried to regain control of the conversation. "You were explaining how you injured yourself in lion form. Continue."

"It was the same thing. I tried and tried and tried—"

Hugh roared and bared his teeth, unable to contain his anger at what would have happened if the Siphon had succeeded even once in his efforts.

Apparently noticing Hugh's reaction, the Siphon stopped mid-sentence, rubbed his lips together, and then cleared his throat before continuing. "Anyway, it didn't work, so I thought maybe if I did it as a lion, I'd have more luck." He shook his head. "But I didn't. If anything, I purred louder and healed faster."

Finally some logic appeared. If there was a way to self-heal, Hugh would expect it to be stronger in animal form.

"You were able do that?" Hugh asked. "You were able to take your claw to your own body and slice yourself open with no hesitation?"

Knitting his eyebrows together in concentration, the Siphon looked away, as if lost in a memory. "I can't remember if I hesitated the first time," he said. "It was too long ago."

Lord. Hugh was going to be sick. "When was the first time?" he asked, regretting the question even as he spoke it. The knowledge of how long his life had been at risk was useless, and yet, he couldn't not know.

"The first time as a lion?" The Siphon focused on him again. "I don't know. Six years ago? Maybe seven."

Hugh's heart slammed against his ribcage and his lungs stopped working. When he got himself under control, he said, "And the other?" He gulped. "When did you cut yourself in this form?"

A strange look passed over the Siphon's—*Johnnie's*—face and his cheeks darkened. He pulled the sweater over his mouth. "A few years before that."

That time period meant Hugh's life had been in danger from the moment he had agreed to take in Johnnie's birth pride. He wondered if they'd known all along they were bringing forward a damaged Siphon. Probably not. After all, Hugh himself hadn't noticed until ten days earlier.

"The scars," Hugh said, his mind throbbing with this new, petrifying information. "They weren't fresh." He flicked his gaze from the Siphon's sweater-covered wrists over to his face. "When did you stop trying to end your life and what made you start again?"

"I didn't stop." Johnnie curled into an even tighter ball. "I just tried different things."

Though it was the answer he had expected, Hugh still needed a few moments to process it.

"And the hanging?" he said quietly. "Was that the first time?"

"Yes." Johnnie nodded. "It almost worked too." He rested his cheek against his knee. "I couldn't breathe so the purring stopped and I thought I'd finally—" He sighed. "But then they came in and cut me down so I started breathing again and then purring and it was over."

"No," Hugh snapped. "It wasn't over. That's the point."

On the one hand, the extent of the problem was more

severe than Hugh had initially realized. But he suspected the solution was reachable. Johnnie hadn't felt included in the pride. He hadn't felt like the pride saw him as a person. And perhaps he'd been right.

Hugh looked at the man who had been by his side for over ten years and realized he had never bothered trying to know anything about him. The Siphon was important. He was critical. But he wasn't a regular lion or a normal person. And yet, maybe he was all of those things. The revelation was a wake-up call to Hugh, and he understood what needed to be done to save himself and the pride.

CHAPTER 4

"What's your favorite thing to eat?" Not the most scintillating or meaningful question for getting to know someone, but it was dinnertime and Hugh was hungry so food had his attention.

"My favorite thing to eat?" Johnnie repeated.

"Yes." Hugh nodded.

"Um." Johnnie blinked rapidly. "I've never thought about it. I eat what I'm given."

Which made sense because, as Hugh's Siphon, Johnnie accompanied him everywhere, including meals. And while members of his pride and the prides he visited often asked about his food preferences, they didn't cater their menus to suit the Siphon.

"Well, I want you to think about it."

"Why?" Johnnie asked, genuinely curious.

"Because we eat our meals together and I can make sure to include your favorites when people ask me what I want them to make."

"The pride cooks for you, not for me," Johnnie said.

That was true, but regardless of whom the lions had in mind while preparing the food, Johnnie would get to eat it. And if he enjoyed it, he'd feel more connected to the pride and more thankful for his role.

"They'll ask me what I want and I'll suggest things you like."

"That's nice of you," Johnnie said. He bit his bottom lip and lowered his gaze as a red tint ran up his neck and over his cheeks.

Lions as a whole weren't emotional, so seeing a blush on one of their kind was unusual and unexpectedly enjoyable.

"Johnnie?" Hugh said, amused at the reaction. "What is it you're thinking right now?"

"Nothing." Johnnie licked his lips, looked up at Hugh from underneath his lashes, and then jerked his gaze away.

What did he have bouncing around in his head that made him so embarrassed? Hugh relaxed into his seat, folded his arms over his chest, and stretched his long legs in front of him, crossing them at the ankles. He stared at Johnnie in silence, grinning every time those blue eyes darted up at him and then flicked away. Eventually, Hugh's patience was rewarded.

"I was, uh, thinking," Johnnie started and then stopped.

"Yes?" Hugh arched one eyebrow.

"Maybe sometime when you're not traveling to other prides or holding a meeting or making your visits to the other dens, we could make dinner here." Johnnie paused and then breathlessly added, "Together."

Meals were social events for lion shifters. They gathered to talk, eat, and drink, bonding and enhancing their cohesiveness in the process. As the Premier, Hugh's presence at the table was considered an honor so he was always welcome to break bread with his lions. And with such a large pride, he'd never had the need to make his own meals. But Johnnie's suggestion was enticing.

Hugh so rarely had time to relax, something he couldn't do when he was with his pride, tending to their needs, listening to their stories and concerns, and making sure to convey strength and safety to them. If he ate dinner at home a couple of nights a week, he'd have the chance to unwind. And while he was certain his lions would scramble for the opportunity to provide him meals, whether he ate them at home or with them, there was an intriguing appeal to the idea of performing the task himself. It'd be like having a hobby.

"Yes," Hugh said with a sharp dip of his chin. "That's a good idea."

When Johnnie smiled broadly, Hugh wondered if bouncing from den to den and meeting to meeting wore on him too. After all, he accompanied Hugh to every one of those places. He wasn't working like Hugh, but maybe he also wanted time to unwind.

His decision made, Hugh said, "It'll have to wait a few days because I have obligations all week, but the weekend is free so far so we can start then. Friday we'll make our own dinner."

"Thank you," Johnnie said quietly as he ducked his head.

The happiness in his tone and smile on his face loosened some of the tension Hugh carried in his shoulders. "You're welcome." After looking at Johnnie for a few more seconds, he shook his head to clear his mind, slapped his palms against his thighs, and said, "Time for dinner. Get dressed and we'll head out."

"Okay." Johnnie stood, Hugh's sweater falling to his knees, and asked, "Whose den are you visiting tonight?"

"Amy Young's." Amy shared her home with eight other female lions who didn't have cubs. She was the most senior lion in the den, and therefore, the head of that household.

Hugh followed Johnnie into his bedroom and leaned against the doorframe as he got his clothes out of his dresser and began putting them on. Johnnie stepped into his underwear and pants, slid on his socks and loafers, and then pulled Hugh's sweater off. After folding it and setting it on the bed, he put on an undershirt and a white button-down oxford.

"Tell me again why you can wear those clothes all day with no problem but at night you're bothered by tags and seams?" Hugh asked, this time genuinely curious about the answer.

Looking up from his waistband, where he was tucking in his shirt, Johnnie said, "Um, I don't love the clothes when I'm awake either, but I'm representing you so I need to look appropriate." He shrugged. "I'm focused on whatever we're doing so it's not as bad. It's not like I'm trying to sleep or relax during the day."

"I see." Hugh still wasn't sure he understood precisely what bothered Johnnie about the clothing, but he recognized for the first time that Johnnie did more than sit around all day. If he had ever thought about it, Hugh would have already realized that keeping up with his schedule was a job in and of itself. As they walked downstairs in silence, Hugh thought about what else he had failed to consider.

"What about in your lion form?" he asked once they were in his Escalade, driving to Amy's den.

Immediately understanding that Hugh was picking up the thread of their conversation from earlier, Johnnie said, "I enjoy being in that form, but I don't know how I'd react to clothing on me because that's never happened." He paused and, after a couple of seconds of silence, started chuckling.

An image of a lion wearing clothes popped into Hugh's head and he too laughed. "Can you imagine how quickly we'd ruin our clothes if we wore them in that form?"

"Catching pants on bushes as we run by," Johnnie said, laughing louder.

"Blood stains when we hunt," Hugh said, the images getting more and more ridiculous as he visualized a fully-grown lion hunting an antelope while wearing a collared shirt.

"Rips from climbing trees in formal wear," Johnnie said breathlessly.

"And when we want to fuck, we'll have to bite off each other's pants so then we'll be stuck only wearing a shirt." That picture had Hugh howling. "Like Donald Duck or Winnie the

Pooh or those Chipmunks." He pulled up to their destination, still catching his breath, and turned to Johnnie, who was looking out the window. "Why is it Mickey gets pants and Donald doesn't?"

Johnnie shrugged.

"They both have tails so it can't be that." Hugh unbuckled his seatbelt.

Slowly, Johnnie twisted his body around.

"Is it because of Donald's big feet?"

Johnnie looked at him and it was all the encouragement he needed to continue. "Can you imagine Donald getting those giant duck feet through his pants legs?"

In response to that image, Johnnie snorted. "I don't think it's possible."

"Fine, but what's their excuse for Daisy?" Hugh threw his hands in the air. "She's a female. Why can't she wear a dress like Minnie? The big feet won't interfere with a dress."

His eyes twinkling, Johnnie looked at Hugh. "You're being silly." He smiled softly. "I've never seen you act silly."

Hugh's first thought was to say they hadn't known each other long, but he dismissed it, because while having conversations with Johnnie was a new development, they'd spent many years in each other's presence. In fact, Johnnie likely knew Hugh's moods better than anyone. He certainly had the most firsthand exposure to them.

"Premiers aren't silly," Hugh said by way of explanation, trying to keep a straight face despite the fun he was having. "We're serious, ruthless, and strong."

"I'll make sure to keep your cartoon interests to myself then," Johnnie said, his lips twitching.

"That's very generous." Hugh waggled his eyebrows and opened the car door.

"Not really." Johnnie unbuckled and opened the door on his side. "Nobody talks to me anyway so there's no one to tell." He stepped out of the vehicle.

The statement was made in the same lighthearted tone they'd both been using throughout the conversation, but it hit Hugh in the gut, halting him in place and leaving him queasy. Before he could analyze his reaction or figure out how to respond, the front door of the pride home they were visiting swung open and lion shifters streamed outside to greet him.

"Hi, Premier!"

"We hope you're hungry because Jennifer said you love pasta but Bevy was sure fried chicken's your favorite so we made both."

"And that meant we had to make side dishes to go with each of them."

"And desserts."

He slowly stepped out of the vehicle and forced himself to focus his attention on the pride members swarming him. Allowing them to sweep him into the house, he said, "Jennifer and Bevy are both right. Those are two of my favorite meals." Both females beamed. "Johnnie, did you hear what they said?" he asked as he turned around, confirming that Johnnie was following him. "We'll be stuffed for days."

"Who's Johnnie?" asked Laura Teak, tilting her head to the side and furrowing her brow.

"The Siphon," Hugh answered. He stretched his arm out toward Johnnie, who stood on the threshold to the house, outside the ring formed by the lion shifters. He curled his fingers up, encouraging Johnnie to step into the fold.

Some of the pride members turned to look at Johnnie, while others remained focused on Hugh. He heard a few whispered comments about not realizing the Siphon had a name, but the interest passed quickly. Then he was handed a drink and an appetizer, led to the largest sofa in the living room, and regaled with questions and stories.

Mara Terrence and Ashley Early sat at either side of him and asked his opinion about a new business venture they were considering. Debra Reedy shared anecdotes from her visit with a cousin who lived two states over in a Nebraska pride. And Karina Landis sought his advice about whether she should have a baby or wait a few more years.

Immediately, Hugh got drawn in to his pride's needs. He listened to their ideas and made suggestions, moved with them to the dining room when it was time to eat, complimented the meal, and negotiated a resolution to a disagreement that had been brewing between two shifters who had agreed to put it on hold until Hugh's visit. By the time they finished dessert, he was ready to go home with Johnnie, who sat quietly at the corner of the table, as he had all evening.

"Thank you for another night of great food and even

better company." Hoping he had provided useful information and calming vibes for his lions, he rose from his chair, smiled at the females sitting around the table, and made eye contact with each of them. "We'll do this again very soon," he promised.

"You're leaving?" Bevy asked sadly.

"You never leave this early, Premier."

That was true. Generally, after eating, they all ended up fucking in one of the common areas. Sex was a tried and true method of bonding and unity building as well as a good way for a Premier to release his high levels of semen, so it was a regular part of Hugh's visits with his pride members. He'd rutted on the rug in this den's living room more times than he could count. But despite his balls feeling heavy, he had no desire to screw.

"It's been a busy week," he said. "And it's only Tuesday." He smiled again and then began walking toward the front door, watching Johnnie from his peripheral vision.

"Hugh!" Karina chased after him. "Are you sure you can't stay?" She grasped his arm and ran her palm down his chest to his groin. "After our talk tonight, I've decided to go ahead and get pregnant." She raised herself on her tiptoes and rubbed her hand over his shaft as she whispered, "I won't get to feel you inside me for over a year."

Female lions who wanted to conceive focused all of their sexual energy on the males they identified as potential sires. Although Premiers produced more seed than other lions and, like their animal counterparts, were able to mate dozens of times per day regardless of whether they were in human or animal form, their semen wasn't fertile. Also, unlike other male lions, when a Premier mated in his animal forms, his penis didn't have the spines needed to rake the vaginal walls and trigger ovulation. The physical anomalies in Premiers benefited prides because, if a Premier could procreate, any childbearing lion would choose him as a prospective father for her young, and a Premier's voracious sexual needs and extended life would result in a disproportionate number of descendants and ultimately destroy the diversity in a pride's bloodline.

"I'm glad you made your decision," Hugh said. He hunched down and kissed Karina's forehead. "You'll be a wonderful mother. Please let me know if you need help finding a new den."

There were plenty of homes occupied by females with young children, many of whom had lived with Karina before they'd had their own cubs, so she wouldn't have any trouble locating a new place to live, but knowing her Premier was available to help her would soothe the lion within and make his sexual rejection less painful. After gently warding off a few other suggestive remarks, hugging a couple of the shifters who rubbed up against him, and reminding them about the pride run, which was less than two weeks away, Hugh finally left the den, with Johnnie trailing behind him.

"Thanks again," he said as he waved through the lowered car window. He was happy to see the most amorous lions grouped together, touching and fondling. Relieved that their physical needs would be met, regardless of his leaving, Hugh smiled one last time and then drove away.

CHAPTER 5

THE week proceeded as usual and during every pride activity, whether a visit at Hugh's house, a meeting, or a nightly dinner, nobody interacted with Johnnie. When they had sat in the car outside of Amy's den, Johnnie had nonchalantly mentioned this treatment, but for the first time, Hugh noticed it in action. Or maybe, for the first time, it bothered him.

Johnnie still shared his bed every night, so Hugh could have talked to him about the situation when they got home but the list of things he needed to do for the pride distracted him. Plus, he was trying to figure out what had set off warning bells in his mind when he'd met Dennis Jones's visiting college friend, who'd joined them for dinner at one of the male pride homes on Wednesday. But more than anything, he didn't talk to Johnnie about his interaction with the other pride members because he didn't know what to say.

Johnnie was a Siphon, made to carry a Premier's power so the Premier could take care of the pride. That role was well-known and firmly established long before Hugh was born. But Johnnie was also a lion, a person, and a member of Hugh's pride, and a Premier took care of his pride. Hugh had the sinking feeling that he hadn't provided care for this particular pride member. And now that Hugh knew him, his plan of paying lip service to the Siphon so he would stop his foolish attempts at death had morphed into a genuine desire to address Johnnie's concerns.

Another realization Hugh had gained from the time he'd spent talking with the Siphon was how much he enjoyed having someone to chat with about mundane things. When he needed advice related to one of his lions or wanted a second opinion on how to deal with trouble brewing in other prides, he consulted Berk elders, who were chronologically younger than he was but still had years of life experience under their belts. He had no shortage of lions who wanted to talk to him about their thoughts and worries. But his job required the pride and outsiders to see him as all-powerful. Meaningless comments about life minutia and things not related to the good of the pride didn't fit that image so Hugh kept them to himself. But not anymore.

Hugh had initially resented having to monitor Johnnie every minute of every day because he had viewed it as a loss of what had been his only downtime, but it hadn't taken long for him to see that Johnnie's presence was a benefit rather than a detriment. He was the quietest lion Hugh had ever come across and Hugh never let him out of his sight, so anything Hugh said and did in front of Johnnie would remain private. And whatever else Johnnie had bouncing around in his unique brain, his actions had clearly established that he had no worries about the decimation of the pride or his own death, which meant Johnnie would never care about how Hugh's image impacted him or the pride.

Speaking and acting without censoring himself was freeing. Even better was doing it with someone who seemed to genuinely enjoy the conversation. Johnnie's laughter and rapt attention showed his interest in their chats. Plus, Hugh found Johnnie's idiosyncrasies oddly interesting, even appealing. For ten years, he had been living with a stranger he didn't notice. But over the past two weeks, Hugh felt as if he had a new friend of sorts. An eccentric, suicidal, homicidal friend, but still a friend.

Hugh sighed in relief when they walked into the house on Friday evening. "This was a crazy week."

"It was…different," Johnnie agreed.

"Did you pick out any favorite things to eat?" Hugh asked. Wanting to change into comfortable clothes before starting on dinner, he unbuttoned his shirt cuffs and then began working on the front buttons as he walked through the house toward the staircase.

"Not really. I'm fine with whatever."

Johnnie's footsteps sounded behind him on the stairs and then the two of them walked through the double doors leading to Hugh's bedroom. As had become their habit, Johnnie went with him into his walk-in closet and waited while he changed. Hugh would then go into Johnnie's room while he did the same.

"I'm glad we decided to stay in and cook." Hugh shrugged out of his shirt, tossed it in the hamper, and then unbuckled his belt.

"Me too. I've been looking forward to it."

"Can you imagine going out again tonight?" Hugh shook his head at the mere idea. "I don't know if it's the limited sunbathing hours or the holidays or end of year work obligations, but when the weather gets cool, people get crazy." He hung his belt on a wall hook and toed off his loafers. "During dinner at Percy Milroy's pride house, no fewer than three men talked to me about whether I think it's fair that Van Hartwick's pride house is having a Valentine's party again this year."

"I heard that," Johnnie said. "They want to have one and they're worried about overlaps in their guest list impacting attendance, right?"

"Yes, that's what he said. But I'm managing a pride of almost two thousand lions. Does he honestly expect me to interfere in party planning?" Hugh unbuttoned and unzipped his pants. "Besides, it's October seventeenth! Why are we talking about Valentine's Day?"

Laughing, Johnnie said, "You're right. Maybe you can make a rule that people can't talk about Valentine's Day when we still have to get through Halloween, Thanksgiving, Christmas, and New Year."

"Don't tempt me." Hugh wiggled out of his pants and then shook them off before draping them over a hanger. "They're driving me to drink." He snorted. "Well, they would if I could get the alcohol into my body fast enough to make an impact before I burn it all off." Aside from being three hundred pounds, Hugh had a higher metabolism than other shifters. Those things made consuming drugs and alcohol pointless and also explained why he ran hot. "And they wondered why I wanted to go home instead of sticking around after dinner." He sighed and removed his socks.

Johnnie coughed. "I, uh, noticed you haven't been as interested in spending, um, time with the pride members as usual."

That comment froze Hugh in his tracks. Paramount to his role was that his lions felt important.

"What do you mean?" he asked, spinning around to look at Johnnie.

"Nothing. Just, you know." Johnnie shrugged. "You haven't been, uh, the way you usually are with everyone lately."

The explanation was so vague that Hugh had no idea how interpret it.

"Say what you mean."

"Usually you—" Johnnie flicked his gaze from a spot over Hugh's shoulder, down to his underwear, and then to the floor. "When you have dinner at a pride home...afterward you usually—" He glanced at Hugh's briefs, blinked rapidly, and then grimaced and swallowed loudly. "You..."

When Johnnie looked at his groin yet again, Hugh finally understood what he meant, though he had no idea why Johnnie was struggling to articulate something so simple and common.

"I didn't stay to screw with them." Hugh arched his

eyebrows. "Is that what you mean?"

"Yes. I... Yes." Johnnie nodded, glanced away, and then refocused on Hugh. "Why?"

"By the time we were done eating and talking, I wanted to go home." And chit chat with Johnnie about nothing of importance. "If I'd have stayed to fuck, we wouldn't have gotten home until after midnight." And then they'd have barely had time to bathe let alone talk. "You know how it is once lions start fucking." Especially if he was one of them. As a Premier, Hugh could ejaculate as frequently as a lion, which was a few dozen times a day, but he could do it even when he was in his human form. "Plus, I need to keep an eye on you. I can't do that when I'm fucking."

The talk of sex reminded Hugh of how full his balls were. His body produced high levels of semen and without regular releases, his nuts ached and his testosterone levels rose, making his temper unpredictable. Needing to relieve the pressure, he cupped himself and gently squeezed.

"That never, uh—" Johnnie's gaze was glued to Hugh's moving hand. "I've always been there when you—" His breathing came quicker.

Already, Hugh had denied himself for too long. Once he took the first step toward relieving his physical need, he couldn't stop. He required satisfaction. Groaning, he shoved his briefs under his balls, curled his fingers around his dick, and started stroking.

"Ah, fuck, yes."

He spread his legs, leaned against the wall, and tugged

hard and fast. "Haven't done this in too long."

With so many lions clamoring for his attention, he never needed to jerk off.

"Don't remember it feeling this good."

He took hold of his heavy balls and massaged them as he dragged his thumb over his crown.

"Ah, damn, there already." He thrust his hips forward. "Fuck. Fuck. Fuck!" Ejaculate sprayed out of his slit, shooting over his palm and up his chest in spurt after spurt until hot cream coated him from chin to belly.

"Mmm," he sighed as he lazily skated his palm over his torso, rubbing the semen into his skin. His mind was hazy with satisfaction and his knees were wobbly, something that didn't happen even after he screwed half a dozen lions in a row. "Now, I really need a shower."

He chuckled and took a deep, relaxed breath. After several long seconds, he started regaining his mental faculties and realized he was looking at Johnnie's blue eyes, had been the entire time. And Johnnie had been looking at him.

"Can...can...can I go to my room and change?" Johnnie slowly backed away. "I promise I won't do anything." He thumped against the wall. "You already took all the blades and ropes." His hands flat against the plaster, he moved sideways until he reached the closet opening and then he stumbled out. "I'll be right back."

When Hugh stepped out of the shower, Johnnie was sitting on the bathroom floor, his legs folded against his chest and a huge sweatshirt pulled over them.

"Feeling better?" he asked, glancing up at Hugh while fidgeting with the hem of his heavy shirt.

"Yes. Tension's gone."

The hot shower had helped with that, but the orgasm was the main stress reliever. Hugh had never come as hard and he'd never enjoyed it as much. Usually sex was about emptying himself of seed to relieve an ache; it was more relief than pleasure. But those short minutes in the closet had been all pleasure. Maybe denying himself for a little while wasn't such a bad thing. If he kept rubbing his towel over his dick though, he wouldn't be denying anything, so, with a chuckle, he dragged his towel up his belly, across his shoulders, and over his hair for a quick dry.

"Good," Johnnie squeaked. He cleared his throat and then repeated himself in a normal voice. "Good. Glad you feel better."

"Yup." Hugh grinned. "Now, I need food." He tossed his towel over the hook. "I could eat a buffalo."

"You just got clean," Johnnie said, flicking his gaze away. "Now's probably not the best time to shift and hunt."

"True." Hugh chuckled. "We can save the hunt for

tomorrow's dinner. Tonight we have a refrigerator full of steak." He stepped toward the door and stopped in front of Johnnie. "Need help?" He reached down.

Slowly, Johnnie raised his gaze from Hugh's shins, up his body to his face.

"No thanks," he said hoarsely. "I'm okay." He swallowed hard, waited until Hugh walked past, and then stood and followed him. "I was, uh, thinking of making spinach too. To go with the steak."

"Sure. I'm not picky." Hugh walked into his closet and rustled through his drawer for underwear.

"Not picky, huh?" Johnnie said from behind him, his tone amused.

"What?" Hugh stepped into this briefs and turned around as he dropped his hand down the front to adjust himself. "I'm not. I eat everything."

Blinking rapidly, Johnnie opened his mouth, took in a deep breath, closed it, and then said, "Remember the time you were visiting the Horizon pride?"

"The Horizon pride..." Hugh furrowed his brow in concentration. The Horizon pride was small, weak, and irrelevant. "I haven't been there in at least eight years. Maybe nine."

"Right." Johnnie nodded, a slow grin spreading across his face. "I'd say refusing the meal served to you and shifting into your lion form to hunt for your own dinner counts as picky."

That reminder helped jog Hugh's memory. "I'd

forgotten about that." He groaned. "Who serves a visiting contingent of lion shifters lasagna?"

"You didn't mind the lasagna we had a couple of months ago at Georgia Pilling's pride house." Johnnie's eyes twinkled. "I remember you having seconds."

After a few moments to think back to that night, Hugh said, "That was beef lasagna and it was served as a side dish to a rotisserie chicken."

"The main dish was a roast. Remember how you said it was perfect because it wasn't too dry?"

"Oh, right." He didn't actually remember, but that didn't matter. "The point is, we had meat. The Horizon pride served us vegetable lasagna with sides of vegetables. There was no meat. None."

Johnnie laughed. "Okay, so you're not picky as long as there's meat involved, is that it?"

Hugh grunted and reached for a pair of jeans.

"I'm a carnivore. I need meat. And now that I'm remembering that visit, the Horizon lions were uppity assholes the entire time and the dinner menu was a power play."

He stepped into his jeans and buttoned up.

"Really?" Johnnie asked.

"Yes." Hugh pulled a T-shirt off a hanger and tugged it over his head.

"What kind of power play?"

"They had a history with your old pride and wanted to make a point that they were better than Westgate even after it merged into Berk, which shows their folly because we're a Premier Pride." He shook his head disgustedly. "They'll never come close to measuring up to us."

"Oh." Johnnie squeezed his lips together and knit his eyebrows as he seemed to think that over. "I didn't know about any history between Westgate and Horizon."

Not sure how best to respond to yet more proof of how isolated Johnnie had been from everything related to the pride, Hugh put his hand on Johnnie's shoulder and led him out of the closet and bedroom in silence.

"Did you say something about the history or the power play during that visit?" Johnnie gazed up at him as they walked. "I was with you the whole time, like always, and I didn't hear anything. I'm sure I'd remember if you'd said it."

"I bet you would. I can tell you have a great memory." Concerned Johnnie would trip by watching him instead of looking forward but not wanting the blue eyes to look away, Hugh slid his hand to Johnnie's back and kept him steady. "And no, I'm sure I wouldn't have said anything. I wouldn't call a pride out on something like that."

"Why not?"

Hugh didn't normally talk about his leadership strategy because explaining why he did things opened the door for others to question his motives and possibly his actions. The whys shouldn't matter—his pride members needed to trust him implicitly. But Johnnie was different from the rest of the pride. Hugh didn't need to impress or intimidate him, and he found he enjoyed sharing his thoughts with his new friend.

"I don't address that kind of behavior for a couple of reasons," Hugh explained as they began walking down the stairs. Johnnie still watched him, his expression interested, so he curled his fingers around Johnnie's hip, keeping him close as he answered his question. "First, when people are so overtly antagonistic, they're looking for a reaction. Not giving them what they want strips them of their perceived power."

"Oh." Johnnie nodded. "That makes sense." They reached the bottom of the stairs and turned toward the kitchen. "You said a couple of reasons. What's the other one?"

"I'm a Premier. I've been leading a Premier Pride for going on eighty years." He paused. "Seventy years at that time. None of the Horizon shifters had even been alive that long." He shook his head. "A ragtag group of wet-behind-the-ears lions thinks serving us a mediocre dinner makes some sort of a statement about us?" He scoffed. "If they're not sophisticated enough to know the only statement made that evening was about them, then they don't matter enough to waste my time."

Once they reached the kitchen, Hugh opened the refrigerator and got the dinner ingredients. He handed them to Johnnie, who set them on the counter.

"Why did you go to Horizon in the first place?" Johnnie asked.

Hugh brought the butter and lemon to the counter and looked at Johnnie. "My memory isn't as good as yours." Johnnie's straight, brown hair slid over one eye and Hugh reached down and brushed it back. "But that visit was right after our prides merged so based on the timing, I'd guess it was one of the trips I took to send a message that Westgate's lions were part of my pride and under my protection."

"We traveled a lot after the merger," Johnnie agreed.

"Yes. Westgate was incredibly vulnerable when I stepped in. No useful land, no assets, disease ridden, weak lions. The only reason they'd managed to stay autonomous up until then was that other prides didn't consider any of the members worth having. If anyone had seen value in the pride, it would have been taken over by force and, more than likely, all but a few lions would have been decimated."

"But you saw the value in the pride?" Johnnie asked, his eyes wide.

All lions had eyes in shades of brown so a Siphon's eyes had always struck Hugh as strange and unnatural. But in that moment, Johnnie's blue, sparkling eyes reminded him of the sky on a clear day and the lake water during the middle of summer. Not only were his eyes natural, they were beautiful.

"Yes, I saw value in Westgate," he said quietly, reflecting back on that time. "Because to get me to take them in, they told me about you."

CHAPTER 6

ON Saturday evening, Hugh looked out the large picture window in the living room. The sun was starting to go down, the sky filling with oranges and reds. He'd spent the entire day at home, with Johnnie. Not quite a vacation because he'd caught up on calls and emails, scheduled visits to a few prides, and gone over the end-of-month financial reports, but it'd been a quiet slow-paced day nonetheless.

While he had worked, whether in the office or the living room, Johnnie had joined him, quietly finding an out of the way spot to sit, a book always in his hand. The familiarity of Johnnie in that position made Hugh recognize that it was the norm.

"You read a lot," he observed, looking at Johnnie's reflection in the glass.

"Yes." Johnnie glanced up from his book. "It's something I can do wherever you go without being disruptive."

Meetings Hugh attended with other Premiers or pride leaders sometimes began in the morning and ran into the night. When he was home, it wasn't uncommon for the entrance to his office to become a revolving door, with one lion after another coming to share concerns and fears and seek advice and for the lion shifters who worked for the pride-owned investments and businesses to report on their areas and get direction from Hugh. In the evenings, he visited pride homes, where the routine was much the same—pride members constantly needing his attention. And on the rare occasions when nobody was around, Hugh was busy on calls or with paperwork. During all of those times, Johnnie was there, siphoning Hugh's power, but not speaking or interrupting.

"Do you enjoy it?" he asked as he turned around so he could see Johnnie better.

"Reading?" Johnnie blinked in surprise. "Of course. I meet new people and see new places." He paused and his neck reddened. "I know they're not always real and I don't actually *see* them, but if it's a good book, it feels like I do and..." He cleared his throat, rubbed his palm on his pants, and lowered his gaze. "Yes, I like reading."

"I'm glad you found something you enjoy to pass the time while you're working with me." And Johnnie was working. Hugh knew that now. "Constantly being still and silent can't be easy." Just thinking about spending his days that way had Hugh's muscles twitching.

Johnnie jerked his head up and stared at Hugh, his eyes wide and surprised. Maybe he didn't expect Hugh to understand or maybe he was taken aback that Hugh finally noticed.

"There's nothing else that has to get done tonight and nobody on the schedule. How about we go for a run and hunt our dinner?" Hugh needed to exert energy, to shift and run and stalk. He felt locked up inside, uncomfortable. "I want to stretch my muscles."

"Sure." Johnnie closed the book and set it on the end table before moving his legs out from underneath his butt and standing. "I'll stay close but not too close, same as always."

The innocent comment had Hugh reconsidering his plans for their evening. The Siphon had to stay near enough to the Premier to hold his power. But to successfully hunt, Hugh had to track his prey in silence, something that worked best when he was on his own. So when he hunted, Johnnie hung back at a calculated pace, giving him the space he needed to make the kill but not so much distance that their connection suffered. Thinking about it, Hugh realized Johnnie had to work to accomplish that.

"Don't worry. I promise not to do anything to myself while you hunt," Johnnie said, apparently noticing Hugh's distraction but misunderstanding the reason for it. "I'll keep siphoning your power so you'll be safe."

Though he probably should have been worried about leaving Johnnie essentially unattended while he focused on hunting, Hugh hadn't been thinking about the possibility that Johnnie would take steps to end their lives again. He'd been thinking about how to enjoy the lives they had. Both of them.

"I know you will." Hugh tried to remember details about his hunts for the past decade but there had been too many to make that possible. "Have you ever hunted?"

"Me?" Johnnie asked disbelievingly.

Hugh nodded.

"I'm a Siphon." Johnnie fidgeted with his shirt hem and shifted from foot to foot.

Yes, he was. And Hugh already knew from Johnnie's brief stories about his childhood that he'd been all but locked away because of it. But even if he had been given the freedom to hunt on Westgate's old pride lands, Hugh doubted Johnnie would've been able to do it successfully when their adult lionesses had struggled to find food on that desolate land. And though access to fruitful hunting grounds had greatly improved after the pride merger, Johnnie's ability to hunt likely hadn't.

As a Siphon, Johnnie had to focus on remaining an appropriate distance from Hugh, so he couldn't search for prey himself. The only way he could have hunted would have been if Hugh had stepped aside and let him. Hugh hadn't.

"You're also a lion," Hugh pointed out. "Lions hunt."

"But..." Johnnie closed his mouth, drew his eyebrows together, and crinkled his nose, his fingers still furiously working the now wrinkled bottom of his shirt. "How can that work? I need to follow you and make sure I stay close enough to hold your power."

"I'm perfectly capable of tracking you." Without conscious thought, Hugh stepped toward Johnnie. "It'll be fun."

"Fun?" Johnnie tilted his head back and focused those bright blue eyes on him.

"Sure. I like a challenge." He liked those eyes. "Usually, I'm either hunting prey, in which case I need to be silent and steady before pouncing and dashing, or I'm chasing an enemy, in which case speed matters but sound and stealth aren't relevant. This'll be a combination of both skills."

And it'd give him an opportunity to observe Johnnie in his lion form. He'd witnessed Johnnie shift hundreds of times, but he'd never paid attention, and suddenly, he very much wanted to see Johnnie's human features transformed into his beast. How would it feel to have those blue eyes looking at him from a lion's face?

"Oh." Johnnie bit his lip and lowered his gaze.

"Tell me what's bothering you." With one hand, Hugh plucked Johnnie's fingers away from his shirt and held them tight. With his other hand, he tipped Johnnie's chin up so their gazes met.

"I've never hunted so I'm not sure I can do it."

"Well, that'll definitely be true if you don't try." Not that Johnnie's inability to hunt had been his choice up to that point in his life, but going forward, Hugh would make sure Johnnie had the same opportunities as the other lions in the pride.

"That makes sense." Johnnie nodded, as if in agreement, but he continued nervously chewing on his lip.

"Your lips will get chapped and red if you keep punishing them that way."

"Yeah, they're, uh, always dry, so..." He swallowed hard. "Yeah."

"We'll get you some Chapstick," Hugh said with a grin.

"That never works." Johnnie shook his head.

"No?" Hugh wondered if that was yet another of Johnnie's physical anomalies—like his eye color, purring ability, sensitive skin, and cool body temperature. "Why not?"

"How can it work when it disappears within two days after I get it?" Johnnie shook his head and chuckled. "Anyone who can figure out what dimension Chapstick travels to and how to get it back can become the Harry Houdini of our generation."

Laughing, Hugh said, "Aren't you too young to be a Houdini fan?" He paused and then tilted his head to the side. "How old *are* you? I don't think I've ever been told." Nor had he asked. Johnnie knew what Hugh ate for dinner months ago and whether he had seconds and Hugh hadn't bothered asking a single thing about him.

"I'm twenty-six, I think." Johnnie's forehead crinkled. "I don't know my exact date of birth but I've been with you for ten years and the pride was thrilled when I came into my ability to hold a Premier's power four years earlier than they'd expected." He glanced at Hugh. "The regular age is twenty, right?"

"That's usually when people say a Siphon goes into service, but Siphons are so rare it's hard to know for sure." And Hugh was starting to understand that another reason so little was known about Siphons might be that, despite their importance, nobody bothered paying them attention.

"I've read a few different biographies about him,"

Johnnie said.

After a slight pause to follow the conversation thread, Hugh said, "You're a Houdini fan?"

Johnnie shrugged. "I think it's neat how he could get out of any situation."

With the life Johnnie had led, Hugh wasn't surprised by that answer. He was no longer surprised by a lot of things Johnnie said or even what he'd tried to do two weeks earlier.

"I met him," Hugh said.

"You met Harry Houdini?" Johnnie sounded awed.

Enjoying that reaction aimed at him, Hugh smirked. "Yup. I was pretty young at the time." He thought back. "Barely thirteen, I think."

"So it was the year before he died."

"It was?" Hugh honestly couldn't remember. He may not have ever known when the famous magician died.

Johnnie nodded. "Your birthday's October first and you were born in 1912. Harry Houdini died on Halloween in 1926, so if you were thirteen when you met him, it had to have been right before then."

"That's quick math," Hugh observed, more to himself than to Johnnie. Although Johnnie hadn't had any formal education or, from the sound of it, informal education, he was extremely intelligent.

"What was he like?" Johnnie asked excitedly. He flipped his hands up and grasped Hugh's wrists. "Did you get to watch one of his stage shows?"

Refocusing on the conversation that was apparently

fascinating to Johnnie, Hugh said, "I did. I was too young to take over a pride at that point, but I was old enough to check them out. I was being courted by a pride in New York so I went for a visit. They pulled out all the stops including front row seats and backstage passes to a show put on by their most famous pride member."

He grinned and started counting in his head, barely getting to two before Johnnie exclaimed, "Harry Houdini was a lion?"

"Yes." Hugh dipped his chin. "It wasn't known by anyone outside his pride, but they told me because they wanted me to be their Premier when I came of age."

"That's incredible."

Hugh shrugged. "It's how he was able to get out of his restraints."

"No," Johnnie gasped. "Really?"

"Yup. It'd be impossible to get away with it today because there are cameras everywhere. And actually, it was a bad idea back then too. If anyone had seen him shift, he risked exposing our kind." Hugh shook his head disapprovingly. "His entire pride was like that, though. They were high-level executives working in Manhattan. They had no space to let their animals free and their power as humans had turned into hubris, so they were wealthy in money but lacking in instincts. Their lions were weak."

"Is that why you didn't go there?"

"Yes. A great pride is one with happy lions. Having healthy finances is part of that, but without enough space to live together as a community, to connect with each other, our animals, and the land, our instincts get weak and our souls wither. They refused to acknowledge that." He sighed and shook his head. "Thankfully, we don't have those issues in Berk."

"The Berk lions seem very happy," Johnnie agreed, his tone sincere despite the fact that he himself had been unhappy to the point that he'd used increasingly violent methods to try to end his life.

Hugh worked hard to ensure his lions remained content and safe, but in that moment, he cared about one particular lion being happy. And he was sure using his animal's body as it was meant to be used would fill Johnnie with adrenaline and joy.

"Enough talking. It's time to hunt." He rubbed his palm over Johnnie's back and then kept it in place as he began walking toward the back of the house, taking Johnnie with him.

"I'll try."

"It's instinct." Hugh opened the back door and waited for Johnnie to step outside before joining him on the porch.

"Instinct." Johnnie's expression turned thoughtful. "Right. That makes sense. And I've watched you do it for a long time, so that probably helps too."

So many conversations with Johnnie served as reminders of how close he'd been to Hugh for years, how aware he was of every aspect of Hugh's life, and how, in return, Hugh had been essentially oblivious toward him.

"Watching is the first part of learning," Hugh said agreeably as he unbuttoned his shirt. "But the *fun* part is doing it yourself. Whether you catch anything or not, the hunt itself is the point."

"Okay." Johnnie followed Hugh's lead and began undressing. Hugh was taking off his last sock, when Johnnie said, "Hugh?"

He flicked his gaze to Johnnie. "Yes?"

"Thank you for doing this with me. For doing a lot of things with me these past couple of weeks." Johnnie glanced down and then up again. "It...it means a lot to me."

Receiving praise for being decent to a man he'd been neglecting, if not mistreating, made Hugh uncomfortable. "You don't need to thank me," he said. While he'd spent more time with Johnnie over the previous two weeks than he generally spent with any one lion and he'd invited Johnnie to share his bed for sleeping, something he absolutely never did with any pride member both because he wanted personal space and because he wanted to avoid inter-pride jealousy, he had, surprisingly, enjoyed those thing. "It's been nice for me too."

The hopeful look Johnnie gave him in response to that comment was as unsettling as the conversation. Needing to move into familiar territory, Hugh patted Johnnie's shoulder, said, "Let's hunt," and shifted into his lion form before leaping off the porch.

After trying and failing to catch an antelope and a deer, Johnnie no longer stood as tall and straight, his tail drooped, and his cheeks were pulled down. His inability to trap his prey had clearly demoralized him.

The animal in Hugh normally would have sought out the kill himself, demonstrating his strength and skill. But his goal that day wasn't to show his power or to impress other lions. His goal wasn't even to feed, though he had planned to eat dinner in his animal form. No. His goal was for Johnnie to experience the thrill of the hunt and to have a taste of success.

So rather than dashing ahead and taking over, Hugh trotted to Johnnie, shifted into his human body, and said, "Let's talk for a few minutes." He dug his fingers into Johnnie's mane. "Shift."

Johnnie dipped his huge, light tan face in what looked like a nod, and then took his human form. "I'm sorry."

"Don't apologize," Hugh rumbled, stepping forward until his chest almost touched Johnnie. "This is your first time. Being prey doesn't mean the deer and the antelope are slow. In fact, they're quick and they have excellent senses and reflexes." He reached forward and cupped Johnnie's cheek, curling his thumb under Johnnie's chin, and then he tilted Johnnie's head up so he could look into those blue eyes.

"Lions fail more often than they succeed during a hunt."

"You don't," Johnnie pointed out quietly, and accurately.

"I'm a Premier. I'm faster, bigger, and stronger than other lions. And I've been doing this for over a century."

Hugh would have suggested that Johnnie consider how other lions hunted, but Johnnie wouldn't know about that. Whether during a solo hunt or a group hunt, Johnnie's entire focus had to be on Hugh. And while all lions had the opportunity to learn by watching their Premier, their main lessons came from their mothers and their peers from the time they were cubs. Johnnie hadn't had the benefit of either.

"Tell me what you did out there," Hugh said.

"What I did?"

"Yes. You were quiet, hunched down, saw the deer, and then what?"

"Uh." Johnnie drew his eyebrows together thoughtfully. "I went after it."

"How?"

"I don't understand what you mean. I saw the deer and then I took a deep breath and ran."

"There was a herd of them."

"Yes."

"How did you decide where to go?" When Johnnie continued to look at him blankly, Hugh elaborated. "An *average* hunter sees a herd and runs blindly toward it, hoping to be faster than at least one deer." He paused and looked at Johnnie, waiting to make sure he was listening before continuing. When Johnnie nodded, Hugh said, "A *good* hunter identifies his target before leaving his hiding place. Then he goes straight for the target. No distractions, no hesitations."

"That's what you do?" Johnnie asked.

"No." Hugh grinned as he rubbed his thumb back and forth under Johnnie's chin. "I'm not a good hunter. I'm a *great* hunter."

Smiling, Johnnie said, "What does a great hunter do?"

"A great hunter still identifies his target before leaving his hiding place. But unlike a good hunter, who leaps toward where his target is, a great hunter watches and learns enough to predict where his target is going to be and he aims there."

"Where his target is going to be..." Johnnie blinked up at him. "How do you do that?"

"I consider all the factors. The direction of the wind. Where the sun or moon are in the sky. All the ways the herd can run. Where each deer is among the others and how they'll all move as a group as well as individually. Depending on where I am, some prey will be more vulnerable than others. That's how I decide who I'll hunt."

"So when you go after prey, you target a specific deer based on where you are in relation to that location, and you don't aim for where they are, you aim for where they'll be after they hear you coming?"

"Exactly. Hunting isn't just about strength and speed. It takes a lot of experience watching patterns for different prey in different areas and at different times of the day. If you pay attention and use your body and your brain"—Hugh tapped his fingertips on Johnnie's temple—"you'll be a great hunter."

Johnnie absorbed that information, his expression turning from ashamed and disappointed to thoughtful and then hopeful.

"Are you ready to try again?" Hugh asked.

"I'd like to." Johnnie gazed into Hugh's eyes. "I may not catch anything but I'd like to learn."

Hugh moved his hand to Johnnie's nape and gave him a squeeze. "You will." Because Hugh would spend as much time as Johnnie needed to make sure of it.

CHAPTER 7

"Percy, good to see you." Hugh stood in Percy Milroy's entryway while the husky, good-natured, and unexpectedly nude man rubbed up against him.

Lions were tactile, relishing touch, taste, and scent, so they were regularly affectionate. Because they shifted together and fucked together, public nudity was common. But there was a line between a warm, friendly hello before dinner and naked dry-humping, and Percy had moved past that line. Hugh opened his mouth to ask about the unusual greeting when the sound of groans filtered in from the next room, disrupting his train of thought.

"Harder," Dennis Jones begged. "Yes, Larry. Fuck me harder!"

It sounded like Dennis's visiting friend was still in town and they were enjoying themselves in the living room before dinner.

Percy stretched up and licked the base of Hugh's neck. The sound of sex, scent of need, and feeling of hot, hard flesh moving against him sent a twinge to Hugh's groin, but it was just that—a twinge. And it was overpowered by an unfamiliar feeling Hugh couldn't quite identify. A feeling that drove him to step back, putting space between Percy's erection and his thigh.

"What's going on?" Hugh asked.

His eyes dilated, nipples pebbled, and dick arching against his stomach, Percy whimpered. "Premier." He reached toward Hugh's groin.

Careful not to hurt the lion, Hugh grasped his biceps and pushed him an arm's length away. His arms were longer than Percy's, so with them extended, Percy couldn't make contact with him.

"Percy, what are you doing?" Hugh asked tersely.

"Trying to take care of you."

Group sex was very frequent, particularly among lions who lived together, so when Hugh was invited to share a meal with lions in a Berk den, he was always welcome to join them for fucking late into the night. But the level of aggression Percy was displaying with him was out of the ordinary. More than that, it wasn't welcome.

"The invitation I accepted was for dinner," Hugh said gruffly.

"I know." Percy curled his palm over Hugh's wrist and tugged. "But we've seen how busy you've been and we want to help."

Hearing that Percy's actions stemmed from his yearning to please him, Hugh relaxed and let Percy pull him into the living room. Members from two pride homes filled the space—those who lived with Percy and those who lived in Georgia Pilling's den. They were clustered in groups of two or more, sucking, licking, stroking, and fucking. Lion shifters were bent over furniture, splayed wide on the floor, and riding each other on all available seating.

"The last time you came for dinner, you didn't stay to let us help you afterward. I heard the same thing from the others. You've been so busy taking care of us." Percy slid close to Hugh again, groped his flaccid dick through his pants, and then reached for his zipper as he sunk to his knees. "So we thought you'd rather have us take care of you than eat."

Emptying his semen wasn't a speedy endeavor for Hugh. Although he enjoyed the soft, wet feeling of a mouth or the tight friction provided by a fist, they rarely pulled an orgasm from him. Hugh needed to fuck to find release and he could go through a half dozen lions before coming.

"It isn't necessary," Hugh said as he yanked Percy to his feet. Based on the wide-eyed look Percy gave him, he had surprised the other lion as much as he had surprised himself. "I'm not in need," he explained.

It wasn't a lie. Though his nuts ached, hanging heavy and full, he wasn't hard. Generally, Hugh didn't masturbate other than during long trips when stress and displays of his power built up his testosterone and seed to unbearable levels and long meetings prevented him from finding release with other lions. But his interlude with Johnnie, when he had taken himself in hand, had satisfied him more than multiple nights of fucking, so he wasn't in danger of acting irrationally or violently. And sexual need aside, Hugh found he had no desire to join the rutting lions in front of him.

"Don't you want us to take care of you?" Percy asked, confusion and worry mapped across his face. "You must be hurting with nobody fulfilling your need." He reached for Hugh's dick and, once again, Hugh stopped him.

"I'm fine."

Sexually, he was fine. Emotionally, he was confused about the change in his own desires and frustrated with his pride members setting him up. Manipulation was a form of aggression and Hugh wouldn't allow it. But because it was completely out of character for his lions to challenge him, he was willing to limit the discipline to whoever had orchestrated the unannounced change in plans.

"Was this your idea, Percy? Did you decide to invite people from Georgia's pride home here and then replace the meal with this?" To indicate his meaning, Hugh tilted his chin across the roomful of screwing shifters. He caught sight of Johnnie in the corner. Like always, he had done his job silently, following behind Hugh and remaining close enough to siphon Hugh's power. With his shoulders hunched, hands in his pockets, and gaze locked on the floor, he looked as uncomfortable as Hugh felt.

As Hugh stared at him, Johnnie looked up and their gazes locked. Protecting his pride, keeping them safe and fulfilled, those were typical emotions for Hugh, and he recognized them soul deep, so he knew they weren't the drivers of the sudden and sharp desire to march over and fix whatever had taken away the happy smile Johnnie had worn during their drive over.

"It was my idea, Hugh," said an unfamiliar voice, pulling his focus away from woeful but mesmerizing blue eyes.

Hugh glanced down to see Dennis Jones's visiting friend on his hands and knees, crawling toward him. In lion form, that would have made sense, but he was in his human skin.

"Larry Ridley, right?"

"You remember me." Larry licked his lips. "I'm glad I made a good impression."

Actually, it was the opposite. Something about the lion had raised Hugh's hackles from the moment they'd met.

"And I see I'm impressing you again." He dragged his palm over Hugh's shoe, underneath his pants hem, and up his leg as he raised his head and rubbed his cheek against Hugh's inner thigh seductively. "You're hard for me, Hugh." He rose to his knees, tipped his head up, and mouthed Hugh's shaft through his pants.

"Premier," Hugh bit out as he jerked away, removing Larry's support and leaving him scrambling to find his balance. The visiting lion was in no way arousing, and he wasn't the cause of Hugh's erection.

"What?" Larry stared up at him.

"You may address me by my title," Hugh clarified. "I'm a Premier."

"But Dennis calls you—"

"Dennis is one of my lions. He's in my pride and I've invited him to use my name." Hugh bared his teeth, flared his nostrils, and growled. "I didn't give you permission to do that. Just like I didn't give you permission to touch me. You haven't earned those privileges." He glared at Larry. "You're a friend of Dennis's so I'll let the transgression go this one time. Don't do it again."

"Hugh?" Percy said, his eyes wide as he darted his gaze back and forth between Hugh and the lion still kneeling at his feet. "I'm sorry. We thought we were helping. Are you angry?"

Yes, he was angry. And frustrated. And confused. His dick was hard but he was uncharacteristically repelled by the idea of joining the orgy going on in front of him.

"You're fine, Percy," Hugh said, hoping his tone was soothing. He kept his voice low enough for Percy's ears alone so he wouldn't embarrass or disrupt the other lions. "I have been working hard and I appreciate your desire to help me, but if I need something from you or the rest of the pride, I will say so. Don't make assumptions."

Percy nodded furiously. "Of course. I didn't mean…we didn't mean…"

"I understand this wasn't your idea but I expect more from my pride. I will not be manipulated or second-guessed. If I say I want to go to my home after a meal, that is what I mean. Nothing more, nothing less. Changing plans without telling me because you think it's what I need isn't acceptable."

Percy trembled, remorse rolling off him in waves.

"Mistakes are part of life. Making them is normal." Hugh locked a steely gaze on Percy. "Repeating them once you've been taught otherwise, however, is not."

When Percy whimpered and looked at Hugh beseechingly, Hugh rumbled low in this throat, cupped Percy's nape, and pulled him forward.

"You're forgiven." He rubbed his chin over Percy's head, scent-marking him and sending a message of acceptance.

"Thank you." Percy sighed in relief.

With another approving rumble, Hugh released Percy and moved away.

"I'm leaving now."

"I can get some of the others and we can quickly make you a meal," Percy said.

"No." Hugh shook his head. "They're enjoying themselves and I'm able to fend for myself in my kitchen."

Though he looked disappointed, Percy nodded without argument. "I'm sorry, Premier."

Hugh dipped his chin, squeezed Percy's shoulder, and then turned around and marched out of the room, his focus on the quiet lion who, like always, trailed after him.

They drove home in silence but Johnnie's nonverbal cues communicated how he felt. As soon as he'd realized they were leaving, he'd removed his hands from his pockets, slowly straightened his shoulders, and held his head higher. While they drove, he'd stopped clenching his jaw and the tightness had disappeared from the corners of his eyes. By the time they pulled into the garage, Johnnie was breathing slower and calmer.

Clearly, Johnnie felt better. Hugh did too. But he didn't understand why he had been so intensely uncomfortable at Dennis Jones's pride house. Anger at his lions' actions made sense, but that wasn't what had driven him to leave. Hugh put the car in park, took the keys out of the ignition, and then rolled his head to the side and appraised the man sitting beside him.

"You must be hungry," Johnnie said.

"A little." More than anything, Hugh was distracted. Something had changed and he couldn't put his finger on what it was.

"We have cold cuts and bread. Are you okay with sandwiches for dinner?"

"Sure."

The mood subdued but not awkward, they walked into the house and headed for the kitchen. Johnnie went straight for the breadbox on the counter, taking out a ciabatta loaf. Hugh opened the refrigerator and got out meat slices, cheese, and mayonnaise. They worked in concert, assembling their meal with the easy familiarity they'd built over the previous three weeks.

"Milk?" Johnnie asked once the sandwiches were plated.

"Yes." Hugh always drank milk with his sandwiches. Johnnie, on the other hand, drank tea.

A couple of minutes later, Johnnie set a glass of milk in

front of Hugh and a mug of tea in front of his own plate. He sat down, picked up his sandwich, and munched happily.

Hugh watched the way he curled his fingers over the bread, how he occasionally darted his pink tongue out to lick the sides of his mouth, and how he sighed contentedly when he sipped his tea.

"Is that sandwich okay?" Johnnie asked, tilting his head toward Hugh's uneaten food.

Glancing down at Johnnie's plate, Hugh noticed it was empty while his own was untouched. "Sure." He picked up the sandwich, took a bite, and chewed by rote, not registering the flavor.

"I'll clean up." Johnnie tilted his head to the side, bit his lip, and drew his eyebrows together as he looked at Hugh. "You're sure you're okay?"

"Yes." No.

When Johnnie leaned over him and took his empty plate, Hugh realized two things. He was done eating and Johnnie smelled good. Really good.

"Maybe we should go to bed early," Johnnie suggested. "You seem like you're hurting."

Not in the way Johnnie meant, but if he didn't take care of the hardness between his legs soon, he would be.

"Ready?" Johnnie stepped over and laid a gentle hand on Hugh's shoulder. "Hugh?"

"I'm fine." Hugh stood.

With a hesitant nod, Johnnie moved aside and then followed Hugh up the stairs and into the bedroom. When they got inside, Hugh turned around and dragged his gaze over the other lion.

"You're scaring me," Johnnie said quietly.

Rearing back, Hugh said, "You think I'll hurt you?"

"No." Johnnie shook his head quickly. "I'm scared you're hurt or sick or—" He sighed. "You're acting different."

"Well, you look different."

"Me?"

Dragging his gaze from Johnnie's head, down his body, and back up again, Hugh nodded. "Yes."

Maybe Johnnie had done something slight and Hugh's subconscious had registered it. Would that explain the unfamiliar feelings coursing through him?

"What did you change?"

"Nothing." Johnnie tapped his palms over his blue button-down shirt, tan pants, and then the sides of his face and hair. "I'm exactly the same."

But he wasn't. Hugh didn't remember Johnnie's jawline being as strong, his cheekbones as high, or his lips as red and plump. His brown hair looked softer and had it always been streaked with gold highlights? He didn't recall his skin being so clear that it nearly glowed. And it was difficult to know for certain with Johnnie clothed, but he'd never noticed the broadness of his chest, tightness of his waist, and the enticing bulge in his pants.

The last thought made Hugh gasp. "What happened tonight?" he said quietly, not sure if he was directing the question at Johnnie or himself.

"Tonight?" Johnnie screwed his eyebrows together. "Uh, Percy Milroy, or the people in his den, invited the people in Georgia Pilling's den over for sex instead of preparing dinner for you."

Johnnie had answered the literal question posed to him, but it wasn't the question Hugh had asked.

"And I didn't join them," Hugh said quietly, thinking over that fact and how unusual it was. Or at least how unusual it used to be. He took a moment to reflect. It had been nearly three weeks since the last time he'd screwed anyone.

"I was wondering about that," Johnnie said quietly. "Why didn't you join them?"

"You didn't either," Hugh snapped, feeling as if he had to defend himself, if not from Johnnie's comment then from the unfamiliar feelings and thoughts swirling through him.

"But usually you do." Johnnie paused and then, as if reading Hugh's mind, said, "But not lately."

Hugh opened his mouth to once again point out that the same thing applied to Johnnie because he hadn't had sex lately either and then a realization struck him. He had never, in the ten years he had lived with Johnnie, seen him fuck. For that matter, he hadn't thought of him sexually, which was why he was so taken aback by the lust he had felt when he looked at Johnnie's groin.

The Siphon had always been the Siphon. But as Hugh ran his gaze over Johnnie's sharp features and strong body, he saw a man. A smart, funny, kind, sexy man who made his nuts throb and not because of biology, but because of desire.

"What's wrong with me?" he said.

"Are you feeling sick?" Johnnie asked, misunderstanding Hugh's comment. He stepped up to Hugh until their torsos nearly connected, reached up, and flattened his hand on Hugh's forehead. "You don't feel feverish." Blue eyes examined Hugh worriedly.

Surely he had gone too long without sex, because when Johnnie touched him, Hugh's stomach tightened and his dick hardened to a level that normally required intense foreplay and a long bout of fucking. Wanting to experience the scent he'd noticed in the kitchen again, Hugh inhaled deeply.

Johnnie smelled of citrus and lavender. It wasn't cologne. Johnnie was with him continuously so Hugh knew he didn't use any. He also knew Johnnie's soap was the same unscented brand he used, their clothing was laundered together, and they hadn't eaten or been around either of those plants. That meant the delicious aroma was natural to Johnnie. Hugh moaned.

"Hugh? Do you hurt?"

He ached, but not in an unpleasant way.

"You smell..." Different wasn't the right description. That scent wasn't new; it was familiar. And Hugh enjoyed that familiarity.

"I smell bad?" Johnnie plucked his shirt up to his nose and inhaled. "I don't smell anything."

"No, not bad," Hugh rasped.

"Maybe I got something on me." Johnnie feverishly yanked at his buttons and then pulled his dress shirt off, leaving him wearing only his fitted white undershirt. He tossed the garment aside, leaned forward, and said, "Is that better?"

The way the thin cotton fabric hugged Johnnie's chest made Hugh dizzy.

"What is it?" Johnnie kicked off his shoes and then wiggled out of his pants, throwing them in the same direction as his shirt. "I've never seen you get sick."

"It's not your clothes," Hugh husked, his already deep voice going so low it was unfamiliar to himself. "It's you."

"I swear, I didn't touch anything." Johnnie moved away frantically. "I'll shower."

Before Hugh could explain, Johnnie stripped out of his undershirt and briefs. He bent down to peel off his socks, tilting his firm, pale ass up invitingly, and decimating Hugh's speaking ability.

"I'll get these clothes out of here." Johnnie scooped everything up and cradled it in his arms, leaving his lower half exposed.

Immediately, Hugh dropped his gaze. Johnnie's cock was pink and smooth. It draped slightly to the left over nicely sized balls. As he dashed across the room, it swung enticingly.

"Hugh?"

Hugh jerked his gaze up.

"You need to come with me."

Johnnie hurried out the door, and Hugh watched him, gaze glued to his ass once again.

Stopping at the top of the stairs, Johnnie looked over his

shoulder at Hugh and said, "The laundry room's downstairs. That's too far for me to go from you."

Right. Johnnie wouldn't be able to Siphon Hugh's power from the other side of the house so Hugh had to stay close to him. Too distracted with his own thoughts and feelings to remember there was nothing wrong with Johnnie's clothing so neither of them had to leave the bedroom, Hugh said, "I'll follow you."

If nothing else, he'd have a nice view. Reflexively, he dropped his gaze to Johnnie's backside, and noted small dimples at the tops of his cheeks. Strike that. The view was great.

CHAPTER 8

"Are you still up?" Hugh asked. Johnnie shivered less when he slept so based on the intense trembling at the other end of the bed, Hugh suspected he was awake, but he kept his voice low in case he was mistaken.

"Uh-huh." Johnnie wiggled underneath the blanket and then popped his head out. "What's wrong? Are you feeling sick again?"

"I wasn't sick." But he couldn't explain the way he'd reacted to Johnnie's scent. The way he was still reacting. "Tell me something."

"Sure." Johnnie looked at him expectantly, his expression open.

"Have you ever fucked?"

"Uh..." Johnnie swallowed hard, and even in the dim light of the room, Hugh could see his cheeks darken. "No," he answered, his voice high-pitched.

The question was simple, the words common. Johnnie was younger than him, but then, so was everyone except a few other Premiers, and spending over a decade as Hugh's Siphon, meant Johnnie had witnessed a lot of sexual activity. Yet, suddenly Hugh felt as if he'd said something vulgar. He had asked the question merely from idle curiosity; he should let it go.

"Why not?" He couldn't let it go.

Johnnie rubbed his lips together, licked them, and then rubbed them again. "I'm a Siphon," he eventually said, uttering each word slowly.

"What does that have to do with anything?" Hugh sat up, the discussion making him too restless to lie down. It wasn't as if Johnnie couldn't get it up, something Hugh knew because he had started noticing the other man's erections in his pants and under the sheets. "You're also a man."

"That's..." Johnnie cleared his throat and blinked rapidly. "That's really nice," he rasped.

"I'm not being nice. I'm just stating a fact." Hugh dragged his hand over his chest in frustration. Okay, maybe his curiosity wasn't idle.

"That's what's nice about it." Johnnie flicked his gaze to Hugh's hand and then back to his face. "That you think so." He bit his lip, looked away, and whispered, "Thank you."

"That I think so?" Hugh curled his fingers around his neck and dug his fingertips into his nape, massaging tense muscles. "What does that mean?" Before Johnnie could respond, he said, "Is that why you don't have sex? Because you think we don't see you as a man?"

Slowly, Johnnie raised his gaze. "We?" he said quietly. "You really think anybody sees me? They don't even talk to me and you think they want to touch me?"

There was no denying the way Johnnie had been

ignored most of his life. Maybe even all of his life. But that had changed. Or at least it had when it came to Hugh. He noticed Johnnie now. Hell, he couldn't *not* notice him.

"Me," Hugh said roughly. "*I* see you."

Drawing his eyebrows together, Johnnie looked at him evenly and said, "What do you see?"

Plump lips. A pink tongue. Silky hair. Soft skin. Entrancing eyes.

"You're trembling," Hugh answered. "Even under that blanket with all those clothes on, you're cold." Johnnie was always cold at night. But Hugh wasn't. He was burning up. "Here." Hugh reached his arms out as he lay down on his side beside Johnnie. "Get close to me. My body heat will help."

Within moments, Johnnie was wrapped in his arms, his soft skin brushing against Hugh's chest, his silky hair caressing the underside of Hugh's chin, and his pretty mouth blowing fast bursts of air against Hugh's nipple. Very fast.

"You're breathing too quickly." Hugh pulled Johnnie closer and flung his leg around Johnnie's thighs, curling around the other lion in an attempt to surround him with heat.

"Oh," Johnnie said, his voice cracking. He grasped at Hugh's shoulders, his chest, and his flank. "Oh."

"What is that?" Hugh rolled sideways, putting Johnnie on his back, and then climbed on top of him. He braced his legs on either side of Johnnie and planted his forearms on the bed to help distribute his weight, but he otherwise kept their bodies connected. "Why do you shake like that?"

"You're hard." Johnnie's voice was a broken whisper. "I can feel you."

"I haven't fucked in weeks," Hugh explained easily. "And that little scene earlier tonight reminded me that my body needs release." Not the orgy at Percy Mitchell's den, but the sight of Johnnie stripping off his clothes and his clean citrusy scent.

"Do you..." Johnnie tilted his head back and looked at Hugh, meeting his gaze. "Do you want me?" He blinked, licked his lips, and said, "I mean, do you want me to help you?" He breathed in deeply and cleared his throat. "With your release. I can help." He bit his upper lip. "If you want."

It was an offer Hugh received daily and, more often than not, one he accepted without hesitation, but as he gazed down at Johnnie's innocent face, he didn't think of the ache in his dick and the pressure in his balls.

"Is that what you want?" he asked. "Because I'm fine. You do a lot for me already." Hugh paused and thought about everything Johnnie had told him about his life, everything he now noticed on his own. "You do a lot for our entire pride. Satisfying me isn't one of your duties."

"You let everyone else satisfy you," Johnnie said softly. "Does that mean it's their duty?"

"They're not doing it out of obligation." Hugh considered the way other lions responded to him physically. "They enjoy our time screwing."

In fact, they seemed to enjoy it more than Hugh. For him, sex served a need. It emptied his body of semen and evened out his hormones and temperament. But relief wasn't the same as pleasure, which was something he'd discovered a week earlier when he'd brought himself to a fast, but delicious climax while staring at Johnnie.

"I don't feel obligated." With his gaze locked on Hugh's face, Johnnie slowly moved his palm down Hugh's side, pushed it between their bodies, and slid it against his erection. "You're even hotter here," he said as he brushed his fingers against Hugh's cock.

The tentative, barely-there touch had Hugh throbbing faster than the most skilled blow job. He wasn't sure how long he'd be able to stay still but Johnnie was too untried to take the full brunt of his sexual aggression.

"Tell me what you have in mind," he requested hoarsely. When Johnnie didn't answer, he gripped his chin and peered into his eyes. "Johnnie?"

"Yes?" Johnnie said, his fingers still mapping Hugh's dick, tracing over every vein.

"What do you want to do?"

"What do you mean?"

"You haven't fucked, but you've seen plenty of it. You know how it works. What do you want?"

"You."

"I'm the only one here." Hugh thought of how to rephrase his question in a way Johnnie would understand. "But what I mean is, as far as sex, when you've watched, what turned you on the most?"

"You," Johnnie said guilelessly.

Clearly, Johnnie wasn't grasping his meaning. Thankfully, they were in a situation where actions mattered more than words. With his balls so tight they felt like rocks, Hugh would normally flip whatever lion he was with onto his or her hands and knees and then plunge into tight heat to slake his hunger.

But sex was new to Johnnie. Even touch was new to him. So Hugh had to tread gently if he wanted to make sure Johnnie enjoyed himself. With that thought came the startling recognition of just how much he wanted that very thing. And how his desire to make Johnnie feel good came from a very different place than his normal efforts to ensure his lions' safety and happiness.

"We'll take it slow." Hugh rocked his hips, increasing the fiction against his cock. "The first thing we need to do is take off your pants." He straightened his arms to a full extension and looked over Johnnie's body covered in his nightly uniform of inside out soft sweats, a T-shirt, and a sweatshirt. "Will you be too cold without them?"

"Not if you're touching me," Johnnie said quickly, shaking his head. He tucked his thumbs into his waistband and pushed his briefs and pants down to his knees. Then he wiggled around until they were at his socked ankles. "There," he said a little breathlessly as he shook his feet, presumably getting the bunched clothing off. "No pants."

Smiling at the sweet picture Johnnie made, Hugh rolled his hips and brushed his erection against Johnnie's groin.

"Oh," Johnnie gasped. He clutched Hugh's waist and

stared at him. "Oh wow."

"You like that?"

Johnnie bobbed his head.

"What do you like about it?" Hugh asked as he repeated the motion, dragging their hard cocks together.

"Ungh." Johnnie bucked, raising his ass off the bed and rubbing against Hugh. "You feel good." He moved up and down, thrusting gently. "You're hot and hard and smooth and—" He cried out and stared at Hugh, wide-eyed.

"You're close," Hugh said more than asked. "Good." He was close to orgasm too. Closer than he should be considering what they were doing, but that didn't matter when blinding pleasure pumped through him. "What do you think about this?" Hugh kept his gaze glued to Johnnie's face as he held himself with one arm and circled his free hand around their cocks, bringing rigid flesh together before tugging.

"Hugh," Johnnie breathed out. He flared his nostrils, arched his neck, and raised his hips. "Can I touch too?"

"Go ahead." Hugh lowered himself and lay on his side, taking Johnnie with him and continuing to jack them together.

Immediately, Johnnie draped his leg over Hugh's, bringing their groins into closer contact. "This is..." He looked at Hugh worshipfully as he reached between them and then he lowered his gaze and, with the softest, most reverent touch imaginable, traced his fingertip over Hugh's slit, his crown, and his balls. "It's like a dream."

Hugh was a Premier. It wasn't a part of him, it *was* him.

So he hadn't ever distinguished the motivations and feelings fueled by his being a Premier to those that weren't. It was pointless and meaningless and he'd never thought about trying. But his reaction to Johnnie's appearance, touch, and scent, his bone-deep drive to see those blue eyes light up with pleasure and know he was the cause, were unlike any response he'd had to another pride member. And when Johnnie shuddered and moaned, his breath ghosting over Hugh's lips as ejaculate pulsed from his cock, Hugh lost any semblance of control.

He slammed his mouth against Johnnie's, rolled him onto his back, and ground against him with a desperate fury until a harsh, all-encompassing orgasm rolled through him. It lasted forever, his every muscle and nerve tingling as he licked, bit, and ate at Johnnie's mouth and tangled his fingers in Johnnie's hair. By the time Hugh was spent, he could no longer think and could barely breathe. He thrust his tongue in and out of Johnnie's mouth, first quickly and then more slowly until, eventually, he lapped at red, swollen lips, hoping to soothe any damage he'd caused in his uncharacteristic fit of passion.

When both of their hearts had slowed to a more normal rate and Hugh could fill his lungs again, he grazed his lips over Johnnie's chin, down his neck, and over to his ear. "Tell me you're okay," he whispered and then, drawn by the soft lobe, he pulled it into his mouth and suckled. "Tell me I didn't hurt you."

"You didn't hurt me." Johnnie whimpered and buried

his face in Hugh's neck, getting so close that air couldn't pass between them. "That's the best...anything I've ever felt."

"I'm glad." And he wasn't particularly surprised. Almost any contact would be better than the life Johnnie had led for his first twenty-six years. But that didn't explain why rubbing off with Johnnie was the best thing *Hugh* had ever felt. His mind awhirl but his body sated, Hugh brushed Johnnie's hair off his face and kissed his forehead. "I'm really glad."

They lay together for several minutes, both of them quiet, but eventually Hugh needed to deal with the sticky mess on his hand and stomach. Sighing regretfully about separating from Johnnie's soft body, he sat up.

"Where're you going?" Johnnie asked, sounding panicked.

"Nowhere," Hugh assured him. "I just need to get something to clean us up." He cupped Johnnie's face with his free hand and held up his cum-smeared palm as proof. "Won't take long."

"You can use my shirt." As if to prove his point, Johnnie wiped his own palm on his shirt and then tugged it down and rubbed it against his belly before yanking it off his head and handing it to Hugh. "You don't have to leave."

Chuckling, Hugh took the shirt and swiped it over his own groin. "Now we need to get you a new shirt so you're not cold." He looked at Johnnie's bare chest and felt a pulling in his balls in response to the view of smooth, firm skin. "Two shirts." He tilted his chin toward Johnnie. "Looks like you took off your T-shirt and your sweatshirt."

"I'll be okay like this."

Hugh arched his eyebrows. "You're always freezing at night."

"I know, but"—Johnnie glanced away—"that's only when you're on the other side of the bed. If you keep touching me..." Johnnie trembled and Hugh immediately reached for the blanket and covered him up to his neck.

When Johnnie's lips curled down and his eyes lost their sparkle, Hugh understood his tremble hadn't been caused by the temperature, but was instead a reaction to the thought of Hugh holding him during the night.

"I'll keep you warm," Hugh said as he lay back down and scooted underneath the blanket. He wound his arm around Johnnie's waist and pulled him close.

Sighing happily, Johnnie smiled up at Hugh, molded himself to Hugh's side, and rested his head on Hugh's bicep.

"I've never slept with someone like this," Hugh said, more to himself than to Johnnie.

"You never kiss anybody either," Johnnie whispered, his lips turned up and his eyes closed.

Before Hugh could process the statement, let alone respond, Johnnie's breathing evened out and he was asleep in Hugh's arms.

"I never kiss anybody either," Hugh repeated slowly. He looked at Johnnie's sleeping face, his expression serene and happy, and skimmed his lips over Johnnie's head reflexively. "But now I can't seem to stop."

Hugh's eyes were closed so he must have fallen asleep, but it couldn't have been for long because it was still dark in the room when he opened them. And he was still holding Johnnie. Although holding might not be the right description for what he was doing. His chest was pressed to Johnnie's back, his arm was curled around Johnnie's waist, and his leg was draped over Johnnie's calves, keeping him in place while he humped his rigid cock between Johnnie's thighs. As soon as Hugh recognized what he was doing, he stopped.

Heart thumping wildly, balls drawn up tight, Hugh was uncontrollably aroused. He wouldn't be able to rest without releasing his seed, maybe more than once. Not wanting to wake Johnnie, he kissed his shoulder and started scooting apart from his warm body.

Hugh paused. Three weeks of sharing a bed had taught him that no amount of clothing and blankets kept Johnnie warm. He leaned forward and brushed his lips across Johnnie's nape as he grazed his palm over Johnnie' chest and stomach. No coolness, no shivering, just smooth, hot skin. Need pierced through him, swift and sharp, making him moan. With his cock throbbing and his control at a breaking point, he pulled his hips back and started moving away.

"Hugh?"

Not having realized Johnnie was awake, the whispered

word surprised him. "Yes?"

"Can you... Will you touch me while you do that?" Even without seeing Johnnie's face, Hugh suspected he was biting his lip and blushing.

"You don't want me to stop?" he asked, wanting to be certain in a way he'd never before considered. Normally, he fucked without thought, driven by his physical needs and those of the lions with him. But those lions hadn't spent a lifetime serving others without consideration for their own wants. Those lions had similar, albeit much lower, drives to screw so they needed to get off too. Those lions wanted to help their Premier because a strong, healthy Premier meant their own lives were better. Those lions weren't Johnnie.

With a small shake of his head, Johnnie moved his hand over Hugh's forearm to his palm, wove his fingers with Hugh's, and timidly moved their hands until they were centimeters from Johnnie's cock.

"Keep going." Hugh's throat was thick with desire, his voice gravely. "Show me what you need." He opened his mouth and grazed his teeth across Johnnie's nape and shoulder. "I'll give it to you," he promised.

Taking in a deep breath, Johnnie lifted their joined hands, lowered them to his dick, and then slid his hand away, leaving Hugh touching him.

"That's it," Hugh rasped as he closed his fingers around the hard-as-steel shaft. "Is this what you want?" He dragged his fist up, swiped his thumb over Johnnie's crown, and then pushed his hand back down. "You want me to touch you like this?" He ran his tongue up Johnnie's neck and over to his ear. "Because I'll touch you however you want."

With a cry, Johnnie reached back, grasped Hugh's hip, and pulled, encouraging Hugh to continue his earlier movements. Needing no further encouragement, Hugh thrust between Johnnie's thighs as he stroked his cock.

"Uh, uh, uh," Johnnie moaned. He arched his back and twisted his head around, meeting Hugh's gaze.

The sight of those blue eyes filled with arousal and desire undid Hugh. He slammed his mouth against Johnnie's and cried out as ejaculate erupted from his cock, coating Johnnie's thighs and balls with his scent. Like the previous night, the orgasm went on and on. Hugh was still pulsing when Johnnie came, his hot cream pouring over Hugh's fingers as he shook and moaned.

They were both heaving for breath when Hugh finally slid his tongue out of Johnnie's mouth, his lungs burning. He rubbed his nose over Johnnie's cheek and chin, nuzzled his neck, and nibbled on his ear.

"Hugh," Johnnie sighed, wiggling back against him and sighing peacefully as he rested his head against Hugh's bicep once again.

Not wanting Johnnie to move a few inches, let alone get out of bed, Hugh wiped his hand on the sheet and then used the corner of the blanket to get most of the stickiness off Johnnie's legs.

"Still not cold?" he asked as he draped his arm across Johnnie's chest.

"No." Johnnie rubbed his cheek back and forth over Hugh's arm. "You make me so warm."

"And my touching you like this while you sleep doesn't bother your skin like the seams on your clothes?"

"Nuh-uh." Johnnie rolled over so he faced Hugh and then he snuggled close, fitting his head under Hugh's chin. "The clothes are..." He caressed Hugh's chest and traced his areola. "We never wear clothes as lions, right? It's not all that different in human form." He shrugged. "They're not natural." He pressed his lips to Hugh's shoulder, his collarbone, and then his nipple. "They're not a part of me."

CHAPTER 9

"DID Westgate have a fall festival before we took them in?" Hugh asked as he and Johnnie walked along the well-worn path from the parking lot to the open pasture the Berk pride used for large gatherings.

"I don't remember anybody talking about it so I don't think so." Johnnie shrugged. "But then again, that isn't something I would have necessarily heard."

If he hadn't expected to hear about a festival, he most certainly wouldn't have expected to attend one. Hugh skated his palm up Johnnie's back and rested it over his nape, his fingers buried in soft brown hair. Though they were already walking side by side, Johnnie somehow managed to move even closer to him. His fresh citrus scent curled through Hugh and his chest rumbled approvingly.

"You like hearing the pride having fun," Johnnie said, misunderstanding what Hugh was appreciating and making Hugh aware of the sound of laughter and small feet running over brush.

"They're in full celebration mode already."

"Well, they had a head start." Johnnie cleared his throat. "We're a little late."

In the week that had passed since the first time they'd ejaculated together, they'd come together every night and every morning. That day, they'd been delayed by an early morning call from the Northlands pride, which had been a thorn in Hugh's side since he'd taken in a dozen of their females. The males leading that pride had insisted that Hugh owed them payment in exchange for the females and Hugh constantly reminded them that people were free to live where they chose. If the shifters leading a pride failed to garner enough respect to motivate their members to stay, the members were welcome to look for new homes.

That call had barely ended when Hugh's phone rang again, this time from one of his pride members who wanted to make sure Hugh would make an appearance at his pride house's Halloween party that night. He assured him that he would, just as he'd attend the parties at four other pride homes. After that call, there was another and then another and by the time Hugh was done helping his lions, it was nearly three in the afternoon—time to head out to the Berk Fall Festival. But Hugh hadn't been willing to lose the shared release he'd come to relish every morning with Johnnie so they were late. Worth it.

"We were busy," Hugh said.

"Uh-huh." Looking up at him from underneath his lashes, Johnnie nodded, his throat working. "We got, uh, started late and you were"—he chewed on his lips and flicked his gaze away—"in a lot of need."

Asserting his power over other lions, even on the

phone, brought Hugh's animal instincts to the surface, so his call with Northlands had left him feeling even more territorial, possessive, and aggressive than usual. Add to that the delay of his new morning routine and Hugh was barely human by the time he could touch Johnnie. He all but attacked the other lion, tearing off both their clothes and shoving him onto the top of the desk. Then Hugh spread Johnnie's legs and feasted on his nuts and cock. He licked and sucked, making Johnnie moan, then scream, and eventually cry from ecstasy as Hugh took him into his throat and swallowed down his essence. When Johnnie was completely spent, his skin slick with sweat, Hugh leaned over him and licked the tears off his face as he rutted against his belly, not stopping until they were both coated in Hugh's semen.

"Was it too much for you?" Hugh asked.

After decades experiencing every possible sexual act, Hugh thought he had felt it all, but being with Johnnie was so wholly different, it left even him shaken. He worried the intensity of what they shared would overwhelm someone as innocent as Johnnie.

"No," Johnnie answered, without looking Hugh in the face.

Knowing his sexual appetite surpassed other lions', Hugh tried to rein himself in during their encounters, but keeping his head was almost impossible when the passion reached its peak. The pleasure he felt with Johnnie was unlike anything he had previously experienced and his resulting orgasms were so forceful they drained him more than multiple rounds with other lions.

"Are you sure?" Hugh asked, because no matter how much he had come to crave their time together, he would stop altogether if Johnnie wasn't enjoying himself. "Johnnie?" Needing to see Johnnie's face while they talked, Hugh halted, gripped Johnnie's shoulder, bringing him to a stop, and peered down at him. "I already told you, your job isn't to satisfy me sexually. There are plenty of willing lions." Although, Hugh now found the idea of relieving the pressure with anyone other than Johnnie completely unappealing despite decades of releasing the hormones flooding his system in exactly that way.

"I know," Johnnie bit out, his spine suddenly rigid. "I've seen them all, clamoring to"—his jaw ticked—"help meet your needs."

Over the past month, Hugh had gotten to know many of Johnnie's expressions. In the early days, he had been despondent, but since then, Hugh had seen him excited, happy, intrigued, sleepy, thoughtful, shy, and sated. But this was the first time he had seen Johnnie's eyes narrowed, his nostrils flared, and his lips stretched into thin lines.

"Are you angry?" he asked in surprise as he took Johnnie's chin between his thumb and forefinger and raised his head, forcing him to meet his gaze. "You are. Why are you angry?"

"Premier!" came a voice from behind him.

"Hugh!" said someone else.

Johnnie flicked his gaze over Hugh's shoulder and

immediately started stepping aside but Hugh curled his hand around Johnnie's neck and held him in place. "We're not done here."

"Premier! You made it." More pride members rushed over and shouted out greetings but Hugh couldn't look away from Johnnie.

"They need you," Johnnie whispered, darting his gaze from Hugh's left to his right as he tried to wriggle out of Hugh's grasp.

"They *want* me," Hugh corrected. Johnnie, on the other hand, needed him. "We are going to talk about what upset you."

Johnnie shrugged.

"We *will* talk about this," Hugh repeated firmly. "Does it have to be now or are you okay waiting until after the festival?" When Johnnie didn't respond, Hugh hunched down until his eyes were inches in front of Johnnie's. "Now or later?"

Squirming self-consciously, Johnnie whispered, "They're all watching us."

"Then we'll talk later." He rubbed his thumb across Johnnie's jaw. "I won't forget."

"After the festival we're going to all those parties, remember?" Johnnie said, looking down.

"It'll be a late night," Hugh agreed. "But we're going to be home together at the end of it, just like always." He tangled his fingers in the back of Johnnie's hair and tugged until he looked up. "Can this wait until then?"

"Yes, but..." Looking nervous, Johnnie stopped talking and licked his lips.

"Tell me," Hugh demanded.

"Are you going to"—Johnnie gulped and darted his eyes around wildly—"spend yourself with other lions tonight?"

"I hadn't planned on it." He had planned to make an appearance at each party, give his greetings, and then go home and do what he had been doing every night for the past week—lose himself in pleasure with Johnnie. Although now he was amending that plan to first include a conversation about whatever was bothering Johnnie.

"Oh," Johnnie said on a breath, his shoulders relaxing. "Okay."

"You're okay waiting until later to talk?" Hugh repeated to be certain Johnnie wasn't simply appeasing him.

"Yes." Johnnie nodded.

Relieved that issue was resolved, Hugh said, "I want you to enjoy yourself at this festival." He kept his voice low so the shifters behind him wouldn't hear. "I realize it's still hard for you, but I want you to try."

Arching his eyebrows, Johnnie parted his lips and then blinked rapidly. "I don't understand."

"Bob for apples. Walk around the circle in the cake walk. Play horseshoes. You know"—Hugh grinned—"fun."

"I'm a Siphon."

"And I'm your Premier. Your job is to hold my power. My job is to interact with the pride so everyone feels included and important. We can both do our jobs and still enjoy ourselves."

"I...I'll try."

That was all Hugh could ask for, so with what he hoped was an encouraging smile, he squeezed Johnnie's nape a final time and then turned around and focused on his pride.

Hugh paid attention to his power throughout the afternoon, making sure his connection to Johnnie wasn't stretched too thin. But he had been perfectly comfortable the entire time so he knew Johnnie had been diligent about staying close. He had also looked around for Johnnie every so often to see if the lion was enjoying himself. At first, Johnnie had been nervous, fidgeting as he darted his gaze around the field, but eventually, he had gotten comfortable enough to interact a bit with other lions and even play games.

By six o'clock, the crowd had thinned out—the shifters with cubs had gone home to trick-or-treat in their neighborhoods and those whose pride homes were hosting parties had left to get everything ready for their guests. When Hugh was sure he had made some sort of contact with each of his pride members, he glanced around, looking for Johnnie so they could leave. The sooner they started making the rounds at the parties, the sooner they could get home for the night.

The field where the pride held the festival, and other

all-pride events, was fifty acres of mostly cleared land, interspersed with small clumps of ash trees. With booths, jumping castles, and rides set up everywhere, it wasn't easy to locate one person. Knowing Johnnie couldn't be far from him, Hugh started walking around, smiling at his lions and making small talk, but staying on track.

Eventually, he found Johnnie farther away than he would have thought possible, at the opposite end of the festival grounds, throwing orange beanbags into wicker baskets and laughing. Smiling in reaction to the happy sound, Hugh stopped walking, rubbed his palm over his chest, and watched Johnnie.

"You're the Siphon, right?"

Though amusement booths blocked the person speaking from Hugh's sight, it didn't take him more than a few seconds to recognize the voice: Larry Ridley, Dennis Jones's friend who was apparently still visiting. Hugh had never gotten in the way of his lions having guests on the Berk pride lands. Those visits often resulted in new lions asking for admission into the pride once the guests witnessed the prosperity of their community and the strength of their lions, but there was no chance of him granting Larry admission to his pride. The lion had an air of superiority and arrogance that set off warning bells in Hugh.

"Without you close to him, he dies, right?" The question sounded like an accusation. "Don't you have to stay close to the Premier?"

"I—" Johnnie turned to his right, tension mapped on

his face.

Larry sidled up next to Johnnie, their shoulders touching. "I guess it isn't that close. Listen, I heard you tried—" He twisted sideways, put his mouth against Johnnie's ear, circled his arm around Johnnie's back, and continued speaking.

Between the distance and the ambient noise from the festival, Hugh could no longer hear what Larry was saying, but he saw enough to flare his temper.

"You're standing too close to *my* Siphon," Hugh growled as he stomped forward.

Jerking away from Johnnie, Larry flipped around and made eye contact with Hugh.

"Yes, I'm right here," Hugh said in response to the surprise on Larry's face. "These are my pride lands." He closed the distance between them with heavy steps. "I belong here." He wedged himself between the two men, blocked Johnnie from Larry's view, and glowered down at the interloper. "You don't. Tonight is the last night of your visit. Tomorrow you leave."

Based on the ticking in Larry's jaw and the defiance burning in his eyes, Hugh anticipated an attack or an argument, which he would have welcomed. He had always considered himself a calm and fair Premier whose pride followed him out of respect, rather than a mindless brute who used his physical strength to keep his lions in line, but never before had he felt such rage. Hugh struggled to keep himself from inflicting pain upon Larry, wanting the other lion to make the first move and justify anything that happened as a result. Unfortunately, Larry had enough sense to realize such a move would be his last.

"I apologize, Premier." Larry dipped his chin and lowered his gaze, an action that would have been respectful by any other shifter, but wasn't when he did it. "I didn't mean any offense. I'm not from here so I didn't know your customs."

Though Hugh wanted to point out that the Berk pride didn't have unique customs and that Larry's actions would have been cause for punishment in any pride, he struggled to articulate precisely what had set his teeth on edge. And, more importantly, he could sense unrest from the pride members who had gathered around them. That wouldn't do. Hugh wouldn't allow anyone or anything to cause his lions worry, himself included.

Stepping back, he calmly said, "I'm sure Dennis has enjoyed his time catching up with you. Tomorrow you leave." The point wasn't up for discussion so Hugh didn't give Larry the opportunity to start one. Instead, he turned around, met Johnnie's gaze, and when he saw understanding there, took in a deep breath and began the slow process of saying goodbye to pride members as he made his way from the festival to his vehicle.

"You called me your Siphon," Johnnie said ten minutes

into their otherwise silent drive.

Hugh cringed. "I know how much you hate being called by your title instead of your name." And at first, diffusing a volatile situation was the reason Hugh had made a conscious effort to use Johnnie's name. But as they'd spent more time together, Johnnie had become...Johnnie, and Hugh had stopped thinking of him as the Siphon. "Dennis's friend raises my hackles," he grudgingly admitted. "I wasn't thinking straight." Which was a problem Hugh very rarely had so either he was out of sorts or Larry Ridley was dangerous enough to set off warning bells in his subconscious.

"No. I mean, yes, that's true. But that's not what I meant. It isn't what you said."

Glancing away from the road, Hugh looked at Johnnie and arched his eyebrows questioningly.

"Well, it is, but—" Johnnie licked his lips. "You said '*my* Siphon' not '*the* Siphon.'"

Refocusing on the road, Hugh analyzed that comment. He had learned that Johnnie wasn't one to make off-hand remarks. Which wasn't to say he was quiet, necessarily, just... judicious in his words. When Johnnie said something, it had meaning, even if that meaning wasn't always clear. So Hugh had learned to listen, really listen, when Johnnie spoke and to then think about what he said.

Had Hugh called Johnnie *his* Siphon at the fall festival? Thinking back to that moment, he recalled that he had. Not because he remembered what he'd said, but because he remembered how he'd felt seeing Larry with Johnnie.

"Yes, I did," he confirmed.

"That's different from before."

Once again, Hugh considered the comment. Before Johnnie'd had a name, he had been the Siphon. For ten years, he had been siphoning Hugh's power, so technically that made him Hugh's Siphon. But had Hugh thought of him that way? The truth was, he hadn't thought of him at all. Johnnie— the Siphon—had simply been there.

"You're right," he said, the reminder of how little attention he'd paid to Johnnie for so long making his chest burn to the point of distraction.

"Why?" Johnnie asked after a prolonged silence.

Lost in his musings, Hugh thought Johnnie was asking why he hadn't noticed him for all those years, a question he had pondered several times without finding an answer.

"What changed?" Johnnie added.

Nothing. Nothing had changed. Hugh was busy from the moment he woke up until the moment he went to sleep. Lions constantly vied for his attention, he had a tremendous amount of responsibility, and thousands of people counted on him to keep them safe, prosperous, and happy. Johnnie had been there for all of that, and yet Hugh hadn't seen him. Now that he knew Johnnie, hunted with him, cooked with him, talked about his day with him, and slept with him at night, Hugh couldn't fathom how that had happened.

"Why did you say '*my* Siphon' instead of '*the* Siphon'?" Johnnie asked, reminding Hugh of what they'd been discussing.

"You *are* my Siphon," Hugh pointed out. But for years he hadn't referred to Johnnie that way, hadn't thought of Johnnie that way, and now Johnnie was asking why. Hugh pulled up next to the first pride home on that night's visitation rotation and ground his teeth as he remembered Larry standing close to Johnnie, talking into his ear, and touching him. "Something about Larry isn't right." He pulled the keys out of the ignition and squeezed them so tightly the metal pierced his palm. "The way he was behaving with you wasn't right."

"What does what you called me have to do with him?"

There was something about the look in Larry's eyes, the set of his jaw, and the tone of his voice that niggled at Hugh, bothered him. And the way Larry had behaved with Johnnie struck Hugh as intimate and therefore wrong. Nobody except him should be intimate with *his* Siphon.

And with that thought, Hugh jerked in surprise, suddenly understanding what Johnnie had been asking all along. He opened his mouth to ask about the foreign feeling when Johnnie's eyes suddenly widened in concern.

"What is that?" Johnnie nose twitched. "Is that...are you bleeding?" He quickly unbuckled his seat belt, leaned over the console, and reached for Hugh's arm. "You're bleeding!"

Following Johnnie's gaze, Hugh saw red drops sliding through his clenched fist.

"Let go of the keys," Johnnie said worriedly. "Hugh, let go." He peeled Hugh's fingers open, tossed the keys aside, and carefully examined his sliced palm.

"What happened?" Johnnie snapped his gaze to Hugh's

face while he gently traced the area around the wound with his fingertips. "What? Why are you looking at me like that?"

"You're purring." If he hadn't heard it with his own ears, he wouldn't have believed it, but sure enough Johnnie was purring.

"Oh." Johnnie gulped and then looked down at Hugh's palm, cradled in his lap.

Once again, Hugh followed his gaze. "What the hell?" The blood surrounding the injured area was still wet but the wound itself had nearly healed. As Hugh stared, his skin stitched itself together and the slight pain of his injury dissipated.

"I told you." Johnnie carefully dragged his fingertips over the lighter, puckered skin and Hugh realized the only visual reminder of his injury was the drying blood. "I, uh, guess you're healed." Johnnie turned his lips up in a nervous smile and touched his own neck and upper chest. "All done purring."

Closing and opening his hand, Hugh nodded. "Yes." He stared at Johnnie. "How did you do that?"

"I don't know."

"Have you ever done it before? Other than to yourself."

"No." Johnnie shook his head.

Unsure of what to say, Hugh stared at Johnnie.

"You're okay?" Johnnie asked.

"Yes."

"Then we should get going." Johnnie tilted his chin toward Hugh's shoulder. "They're waiting for you."

The sound of laughter suddenly registered in Hugh's brain. He glanced around and realized happy, costumed lions were clustered around his car, waiting to welcome him to the party. He couldn't decide if he was annoyed at the interruption or grateful for it. Either way, it was time to go to work.

He sighed, reached for the door handle, and said, "Ready?"

"I'll stay close," Johnnie promised.

"Good." And not because Hugh was worried about a Siphon being available to hold his power.

CHAPTER 10

"ARE you up to hunting tonight?" Hugh asked.

A shiny brown lock fell over Johnnie's eyes as he glanced up from his book. Instinctively, Hugh reached out and gently tucked it behind Johnnie's ear.

"Sure." Johnnie ducked his face but Hugh could still see his lips as they turned up into a soft smile. "I like hunting with you."

"You're good at it," Hugh said. Not as good as lions who'd been at it for decades, but for someone who'd only been out a handful of times, Johnnie did remarkably well. His instincts were sharp, his senses honed, and he took advice well.

"I have a lot to learn."

"We have plenty of time." Hugh reluctantly pulled his hand away from Johnnie's hair and sat next to him on the sofa. "We're immortal, remember?" As soon as the words were out of his mouth, he winced.

A Siphoned Premier could live indefinitely, his power growing with every passing day and a Siphon's life continued along with his Premier's, both of them staying at their optimal physical condition. But that didn't make them immortal, something Johnnie had been doing his level best to prove up until a month earlier. Worried he'd made Johnnie remember all the reasons he'd tried to take his life, Hugh quickly changed the topic.

"What were you reading?" He pointed toward the book on Johnnie's lap. "Anything interesting?"

"Yes. It's about game theory."

"Game theory?"

"Uh-huh." Johnnie twisted sideways and looked at Hugh excitedly. "It's a mathematical concept, but it applies to a lot of things. We can even integrate some of the ideas into hunting."

After a month getting to know Johnnie, Hugh was no longer surprised by how bright he was, or how arousing Hugh found his intelligence.

"Tell me more," Hugh said, partly because he was interested in the topic, but mostly because he was interested in seeing Johnnie's eyes sparkle and his face glow with excitement as he explained the latest piece of information he learned from a book.

"Yeah? You really want to hear?" Johnnie asked, his tone hopeful.

"Definitely." Not as much as he wanted to throw Johnnie on the ground and rub their bodies together until they both exploded, but, yes, he wanted to hear Johnnie's thoughts.

"Okay." Johnnie beamed. "The idea is there's a limited resource and multiple people vying for it. If they compete, it's better for the winner but bad for the others. But if they work together, it's better for the group as a whole."

Johnnie looked at Hugh expectantly, so Hugh nodded to confirm he was paying attention. It wasn't easy. Showing his appreciation for his pride members' Halloween parties the previous night had taken longer than Hugh had anticipated. By the time they'd gotten home, it was nearly five in the morning and they hadn't had enough energy to shower, let alone talk or screw. Then they'd been, not surprisingly, woken by a telephone call from a pride member; this one a mother worried about her admittedly rambunctious teenage sons. A visit to her pride house followed the call, after which Hugh had an unscheduled meeting with another lion who lived there and had a question relating to her job for one of the pride-owned businesses. By the time he finished helping her, they had to hurry home so Hugh could take a call with a young Premier who had just started leading a pride. With those back-to-back obligations occupying him, Hugh hadn't been able to sate himself with Johnnie and the desire strumming through his veins made it difficult to concentrate.

"One of the most famous game theory examples is the prisoners' dilemma," Johnnie continued explaining. "Two prisoners are arrested for a minor crime but are suspected of a much bigger one. The small crime can cost them each a month in jail but the big one makes it ten years. They're put in separate rooms and told the first one to confess their part in the big crime walks out free from both crimes and the other one has to go to jail for the big one. If neither of them confesses to the big crime, then they both have a short sentence for the little crime—two months between them. But if one of them doesn't trust that the other one won't talk, or if one of them would rather have total freedom instead of a month in jail, even if it's at the expense of his cohort, then he'll confess. The total penalty will be much worse for the group—ten years—but only one of them will serve it."

Once he finished his rapid-fire explanation, Johnnie took in a deep breath and said, "What do you think?"

Hugh blinked and forced himself to focus on what Johnnie had said instead of on how beautiful his blue eyes looked.

"I think that's a really perceptive description of human nature." He also thought Johnnie was cute when he got excited. He curled his hand around Johnnie's knee and wondered when he had started thinking anybody was cute.

"But it's not just humans," Johnnie said. "That's what I'm saying. Think about when we hunt. A lion sees a herd of deer and goes after them, hoping to catch one. But there's more of them, right? What if they turned around as a group and attacked the lion? Maybe a few would be injured, but it's not likely the lion would be able to kill any of them if he was busy defending himself from the herd."

"Right." Hugh nodded slowly. "But they're prey animals. They don't attack us."

"That's because their behavior follows the game theory concept—each deer is so scared of being caught that he runs to save himself instead of all of them realizing that the whole could be safer if they risked minor injuries to individuals and turned the table on the lion."

"That's true," Hugh said, intrigued. "How do you suggest we use that as a hunting strategy?"

"Well, I was thinking of what you said about running where a deer is going to be instead of where it is. That's the best a lion can do if he's the only one hunting. But if there're two lions, they can time it so one lays in wait in the path of what they think will be the deer's escape route while the other attacks. Then one lion is basically chasing the prey toward the other lion."

"And we have him surrounded."

"Exactly." Johnnie smiled. "Lions will have a much better chance of catching prey if they work together and share the kill. They might even be able to capture more than one."

If Hugh was the one hunting, he wouldn't need the extra help. As a Premier with over a century of power, he was strong and fast enough to successfully trap his target every time. But the strategy would work well for other lions. It'd work well for Johnnie.

"Let's try it tonight," Hugh said. "Do you know which role you want to take the first time? Do you want to attack the prey while I go around to block their path or do you want me to lead them toward you?"

Johnnie drew his eyebrows together and crinkled his forehead. "I don't know if the two of us can do it."

"Why not?"

"We might have to separate too far from each other

when we're surrounding the prey. I was suggesting the idea for you to share with the pride."

Hugh's chest constricted and his throat burned. This man who had spent his life being, at best, ignored by the pride was thinking of ways to help them. How he could have seen Johnnie's desperate act as an attack on the pride, Hugh didn't know. Johnnie didn't want to harm anyone, Hugh now understood, he'd merely been trying to save himself the only way he'd known how.

"What are you doing?" Johnnie rasped, making Hugh aware that he had leaned forward until their lips were scant centimeters apart.

"Kissing you." He cupped Johnnie's face with both hands and wove his fingers through Johnnie's soft hair.

"You want to have sex now?"

Though Hugh's dick was hard, he shook his head and said, "No."

"Then why—"

Closing the remaining distance between them, Hugh brushed his lips over Johnnie's. Fast breaths tickled his skin, making him aware of the other man's nervousness. "Shh," he said, holding Johnnie in place. "It's just a kiss." He laid his lips on top of Johnnie's again and slowly flicked his tongue out. Eventually, Johnnie parted his mouth and Hugh slid inside, tasting and gently thrusting. The motion reminded Hugh of another way he could thrust into Johnnie and his groin throbbed in response. Before he made a liar of himself, he tugged on Johnnie's lower lip one last time, pulled away, and appraised the man in front of him.

Johnnie was still leaning forward, his eyes closed and his spit-slick lips puckered. "What happened?" he asked drowsily. His eyes fluttered open, the blue shimmering in the late afternoon light. "Why'd you stop?"

"To make sure I could."

When Johnnie swiped his tongue over his lips and moaned, as if in reaction to Hugh's taste, Hugh reached forward and pulled him onto his lap.

"Point proven," Hugh said, rubbing his thumb over Johnnie's bottom lip. "I can stop." He could, but he didn't want to so he kissed Johnnie again.

Sighing happily, Johnnie clutched Hugh's chest and melted against him.

This time, their joining was gentler, lips brushing together and tongues barely touching. Johnnie ran his palms across Hugh's pecs and Hugh combed his fingers through Johnnie's hair. When Hugh eventually moved away, he kissed the tip of Johnnie's nose and gazed at his serene smiling face. In that moment, the blue-eyed lion looked completely at peace, as if all his burdens had been lifted.

"You like kissing," Hugh observed as he continued combing his fingers through Johnnie's hair.

"Yes." Johnnie rested his cheek on Hugh's shoulder and petted his chest and stomach. "It makes me feel"—he sucked in a deep breath, trembled, and let it out slowly—"connected to you."

More and more, Hugh recognized how important

connections were to Johnnie. He relished sleeping with their
bodies tangled, smiled whenever Hugh touched him in even
the most casual way, and eagerly engaged in any conversation
Hugh had with him. Johnnie was a dry sponge who thirstily
sucked in whatever he was given, which Hugh attributed to
all the years he had spent without any connections.

"Hugh?" Johnnie looked up at him.

"Yes?"

"Does it bother you?" Johnnie lowered his gaze. "Me
touching you like this?"

"'Course not." A Premier took care of his lions, made
sure they had what they needed. Johnnie needed touch so
Hugh would give it to him.

"Okay." Johnnie's lips curled up at the sides and he lay
his head back down.

The discussion reminded Hugh of the conversation
they'd been unable to finish the previous evening. He pushed
Johnnie's hair off his face again, kissed his forehead, and said,
"Yesterday, when we got to the festival, we were talking about
sex but we were interrupted." When Johnnie's body stiffened
and he flicked his gaze away, Hugh added, "You were angry."

With a deep sigh, Johnnie finally looked at Hugh, but
he still didn't speak.

"Johnnie, tell me what you're thinking." Hugh was
accustomed to pride members who came to him with minute
worries and concerns. There wasn't enough time in the day to
hear everything every lion would tell him, given the chance.
But he had no experience with someone who was reluctant

to speak. "I can't help if I don't know the problem."

"I don't want your help." Johnnie furrowed his brow, looking unhappy at that implication. "That's not..." He pushed his way off Hugh's lap, hunched over his knees, and let out a frustrated breath. "It can't be like that."

"Okay." Hugh said the word slowly as he considered what Johnnie might mean. "How can it be?"

"You're asking me?" He dragged both hands through his hair.

It was that or not understand what had angered Johnnie.

"Yes."

"I'm allowed to say?" He licked his lips nervously.

"Why wouldn't you be allowed to say what you're thinking?" Hugh asked, having no idea what they were talking about.

"I'm the Siphon."

"You're more than that," Hugh growled. To live, Hugh needed a Siphon. He had known that his entire life, so that aspect of Johnnie was undeniably important. But the man, the friend, mattered too; those parts of Johnnie mattered more to Hugh than he had ever thought possible. "I've told you already. You're a lion, a man, and a member of this pride."

"And they're allowed to say?"

"Allowed to..." Hugh was still annoyingly lost in the conversation. "I can't get the rest of the lions in this pride to *stop* saying things to me!" He shook his head. "Enough with this. Speak your mind. If my asking you isn't enough, I'm ordering you as your Premier. I need to understand why you got angry yesterday." He thought back to the words Johnnie had just used. "I need to know how it *can be*."

"You said you could have sex with the others," Johnnie said hesitantly.

"That's right. I've done that for decades and it's fine." A release of hormones. A biological imperative. Not something he looked forward to, like he did for sex with Johnnie, and certainly not something from which he derived incomparable pleasure, but fine.

"I hate it." Johnnie suddenly looked animated, his eyes flashing and his upper lip curled up in a sneer.

"You hate sex?" Hugh asked in surprise. He'd seen the way Johnnie melted under his touch, heard him moan, and smelled his seed. Hell, Johnnie's reaction was half of what made their explorations so enjoyable.

"I hate you having sex with *them*. I hate you smelling like *them*." Johnnie's nostrils flared and his jaw ticked. "Hate it."

"We're animals," Hugh said slowly, considering each word before he spoke it. Why would Johnnie have a negative reaction to something so common, so basic? And an uncharacteristically strong reaction at that. "We have hormones we need to release." Him more than most.

"Not with *them*. You don't need to do those things with *them*. *They* shouldn't touch you that way."

Without warning, Hugh's mind flashed back to the previous evening: Larry Ridley pressed close to Johnnie, whispering in his ear. That foreign emotion rolled through him again, instinctive, uncontrollable, and white-hot.

"But I can have sex with you?" Hugh asked as he heard his own knuckles crack in his tightly clenched fists. "That's what we were talking about, isn't it?" Hugh hoped the answer was yes, because sharp, unexpected need was riding him hard and he was barely able to restrain himself from pouncing on Johnnie. "You're okay having sex with me? Now?"

Without a word, Johnnie slid off the couch and knelt between Hugh's spread legs. "Yes." He set his palm on Hugh's groin, cupping his balls through the fabric of his pants. "With me, the answer is always yes." Johnnie raised his gaze and looked into Hugh's eyes as he caressed and squeezed Hugh's dick. "Always. Yes."

Amazed at how incredible that touch felt, even through his clothes, Hugh gasped. "Damn." He brushed his fingers through Johnnie's hair.

Hands trembling with nerves, desire, or both, Johnnie fumbled with Hugh's button and zipper until he had his pants open, his briefs pulled down in front, and his hot, throbbing prick exposed.

"You smell so good," Johnnie rasped. As if to prove his point, he leaned forward, buried his face against Hugh's nuts, and inhaled deeply. "Mmm." He mouthed Hugh's balls. "I have to taste you." Johnnie closed his eyes and breathed in deeply. "I know you don't like it, but I..." Blue eyes gazed up adoringly as Johnnie lapped at Hugh's sac. "Please."

"That feels incredible." Hugh brushed the back of his hand over Johnnie's cheek. "Why do you think I don't like it?"

"I've watched you." He touched the tip of his tongue to Hugh's slit and shivered. "I've always watched you and you didn't let them do this to you."

"That's because it's a waste of time. I normally need more than a blow job to pull out my seed." And the act itself wasn't normally enjoyable. But sex with Johnnie bore only a cursory resemblance to the activity as Hugh knew it. Draining himself was merely a side effect of the incredible pleasure. "But I can already tell it'll be different with you," Hugh said, his throat thick and voice gravelly as he swiped his thumb across Johnnie's lip.

With an almost pained cry, Johnnie opened his mouth and sucked Hugh's thumb inside. Moaning and whimpering, he felated Hugh's digit like it was his dick.

"Go ahead." He cupped the back of Johnnie's head with one hand, gripped the base of his cock with the other, and painted Johnnie's lips with his glans. "I'm all yours."

Johnnie rubbed his face over Hugh's shaft, bringing him to the brink with just that light contact. Moaning happily, he took Hugh in, licking and sucking, head bobbing, and fingers caressing Hugh's balls.

Usually during sex, Hugh had to force himself to focus and concentrate on his balls and dick so he could push through to the end and come. But Johnnie had barely started and Hugh had to stop himself from going off right then. He wasn't ready for the soft licks and strong suction to end, wasn't ready for Johnnie's happy noises to stop, wasn't ready for those heated blue eyes to stop looking up at him, so he forced himself to slow his breathing, relax, and enjoy Johnnie's ministrations.

New to the sensation of a thick rod filling his mouth, Johnnie couldn't take much of Hugh in at first, but after a few minutes of diligent attention, he was able to go deeper until, eventually, Hugh's cockhead hit the back of his throat.

"Ungh, Johnnie," Hugh moaned. He gently petted the back of Johnnie's hair and lifted his own ass off the couch, the pumping motion instinctive and unstoppable. "I'm going to come."

Rather than pulling away, Johnnie sucked harder and faster, moaned louder, and, gazed at Hugh, his eyes begging.

"Yes," Hugh agreed to the silent request. He thrust his hips a few more times and, with his eyes locked with Johnnie's, groaned as white-hot pleasure swamped his entire being and endless streams of ejaculate poured from his cock into Johnnie's waiting mouth.

"Mmm. Mmm. Mmm," Johnnie moaned as he gulped down Hugh's offering.

Johnnie's entire body shook and the scent of his seed hit Hugh, telling him that the beautiful lion had found his pleasure by bringing him off.

The moment he could muster the ability to talk, Hugh said, "Come up here, Johnnie." He reached down, lifted Johnnie onto his lap, and kissed him ferociously. "That was so good." He gripped Johnnie's chin and nipped at his lips.

"So damn good."

"Thank you." Johnnie bent his neck and kissed the back of Hugh's hand.

They sat quietly for a few minutes, sharing soft kisses and tender touches. When Hugh's stomach growled, he remembered their plans for the evening. "Are you still up for shifting and testing out your new hunting strategy?"

"I'd like to hunt, but I'm not sure we can separate enough to try the game theory concept."

The reminder about the need for the Siphon to remain close to the Premier had Hugh instinctively focusing on the channel that ran between him and Johnnie. It felt stronger than usual. Then again, with Johnnie on his lap, he was as close to Hugh as he could get short of literally taking Hugh inside his body.

Groaning at that image, Hugh reconsidered his plan for the evening. Maybe he could spend himself with Johnnie a few more times and they could eat leftovers for dinner.

No. He shook his head to clear the unusually strong haze of lust.

His orgasm had been intense and powerful. It had drained his seed, sated his body, and strengthened his spirit, same as every release he'd shared with Johnnie over the past couple of weeks. So no matter how good Johnnie looked and smelled, Hugh shouldn't be needy to the point of distraction. Even if he hadn't pushed his cock into a warm, tight hole in a month. Remembering the last time he'd fucked—the night Johnnie had hanged himself—cooled off Hugh's arousal faster than an ice bath.

"We'll shift, go for a long run, and then hunt." Hugh tapped Johnnie's hip and then rose, standing them both up. "If we can't part far enough to test your theory, we'll take down the prey the old-fashioned way."

"Okay." Johnnie leaned against him and closed his eyes for a few seconds and then he sighed happily, straightened, and said, "Let's hunt."

CHAPTER 11

A DECADE ago, Johnnie had been looking out a window and he had seen a black lion for the first time. In that moment, he had known soul deep that his life was about to change forever, that he'd finally be seen, finally be whole, finally be free. As years came and went and nothing changed, that hope had withered and died, but Johnnie's awe at Hugh's glorious beast had never waned. Then suddenly, the future Johnnie had once wished for miraculously became a reality.

Now he could do more than watch the giant lion from a not-too-far distance. He was allowed to rub his body against Hugh's, to lap at his chin and lips, and to wind himself around the other lion. He didn't know what had changed.

One day he had been the Siphon, same as always, there but not, seeing everything he wanted right in front of him, but unable to have it for himself, and spending almost every moment plotting an escape from life. And seemingly the next moment, Hugh had been talking with him, looking at him, and even touching him. The change had been so welcome, so necessary, and so unexpected that Johnnie hadn't let himself question it for fear that it'd stop.

So there he was, on a Saturday evening, stalking

through the woods behind Hugh in his lion skin, diligently paying attention to every scent and every sound. When a faint whiff skittered past him, he halted, one paw in the air. Raising his nose, he inhaled deeply.

There. To the right. Elk.

Hugh must have smelled it too, because he looked back over his shoulder, making eye contact with Johnnie before changing course in the direction of the prey. Slowly and carefully they slithered around trees and brush until they saw a group of elk feeding at the edge of a small clearing.

Following the lessons Hugh had taught him, Johnnie assessed each animal and what route it likely would take in response to an attack from the north, where Hugh and Johnnie were located. The western direction was blocked by a wide stream. Most of the eastern side was thickly treed, with loose, uneven rocks. That made the south the most likely escape route both from a topography perspective and because it was the area closest to the elk and farthest from Hugh and Johnnie, which would give the prey the longest possible lead time.

In deference to Hugh's suggestion that they test out the game theory concept by spreading out—one of them remaining in place and the other standing guard in the path of the escape route—Johnnie considered whether he could get that far from Hugh without risking the connection that allowed him to carry Hugh's power. If he went straight across the clearing to the elk, there wouldn't be a problem. But to make the experiment work, the elk couldn't be allowed to see or scent the lions until they were surrounded. That meant one of them would need to circle around to their endpoint, leaving a wide berth around the clearing. They'd be a worrisome distance apart and they'd have no sightline to each other, two factors that stressed their connection.

Not seeing how that could work, Johnnie looked at Hugh for direction on what strategy they'd employ. Unfortunately, communication as lions wasn't as clear and simple as in their human skin, so when Hugh met Johnnie's gaze and tilted his head to the side, Johnnie was at a loss as to what he meant. Apparently realizing their predicament, Hugh shifted into his human form, the transition smooth, silent, and impressive. Everything about the huge Premier was impressive.

He crouched down, put his mouth to Johnnie's ear, and, his voice barely audible, said, "You go around on the other side of the stream until you get to the southern end of the clearing and I'll chase them toward you."

Though Johnnie wanted to explain that they couldn't get that far apart, unlike Hugh, other lions didn't move from one form to another so seamlessly and he couldn't risk making noise by shifting. Besides, Hugh surely understood that problem.

"During the festival, you were almost as far from me as the furthest spot on that route and we were separated by booths," Hugh whispered.

Widening his eyes in surprise, Johnnie thought about the fall festival. Hugh had insisted that Johnnie have fun, which he said meant participating in the events. The clearing had been so crowded and filled with rides and games that Johnnie had lost visual contact with Hugh almost immediately. But he had stayed focused on their connection all afternoon and never once did it stretch dangerously. Because he hadn't been able to see Hugh, Johnnie didn't realize how far apart they'd gotten so he was surprised to hear Hugh had been more than a row or two away.

In ten years serving as Hugh's Siphon, Johnnie didn't remember ever being able to separate anywhere near that distance, particularly when their visual connection was broken. But if Hugh thought it was safe, Johnnie would do it. He rubbed his cheek against Hugh's chest affectionately and then turned and started the journey around the clearing. He trotted as quickly as possible while still remaining vigilant about the ground in front of him to avoid snapping a loud branch. Unfortunately, all that focus on the dirt and vegetation, distracted him from noticing another lion nearby until he was practically on top of Johnnie.

The sound of steps and cracking leaves registered first and Johnnie initially thought Hugh had discerned a weakness in their connection and was coming after him. He was so worried about the possibility that he had endangered Hugh that he turned and ran in the direction of the sound. It wasn't until the scent hit him that he became aware of his mistake and by then it was too late.

Larry Ridley was leaping from behind a tree, ears flat, teeth bared, and claws extended.

Though he would have liked to roar loud enough to get Hugh's attention and warn him about the danger, Johnnie couldn't. As a younger lion, he had tried to make that particular sound and found he wasn't able to come even close to a roar. So instead, he snarled and snorted as he batted at the lion who had pinned him to the ground.

Claws and sharp teeth dug into Johnnie's skin as he and Larry rolled from side to side. Thankfully, none of the injuries were to his throat and eventually Johnnie managed to get the upper hand. He pinned Larry to the ground and almost had his teeth around Larry's jugular when a piercing pain shot through his head. With a whimper, he slumped to the side and shifted into his human form as everything went dark. Unable to move, he expected more bites, but instead, he was left alone on the cool earth, trying to catch his breath and open his eyes.

"Why'd you do that?" hissed Larry. Apparently also having shifted into his human skin.

"He was about to kill you."

Another voice? Someone else must have approached when Johnnie was distracted by his fight with Larry. He was going to have to do a better job of paying attention to his surroundings.

"Are you out of your mind? There's no way he could kill me!"

"Didn't look that way to me," the person grumbled and Johnnie finally realized it was Dennis Jones.

Why would a pride member attack him? For that matter,

why would Larry attack him? Johnnie's head swam and he made himself stay still. He was wounded and vulnerable and his best chance of escape was Larry and Dennis thinking he was dead. From the force of that hit to his head, he should have been dead.

"I had it under control. Did you have to bash him so hard? And did you have to aim for his head?"

"He was in his lion form. I was trying to stop you from getting killed. How in the hell was I supposed to do that other than hitting him in the head? You should be thanking me that it worked!"

"I'm not thanking you for destroying our lottery ticket. We needed him alive!"

"Calm down, Larry. He's not dead."

"Don't tell me to calm down. He isn't moving and he shifted into his human form. That happens when we die."

"Do we make noise when we're dead? Because the Siphon is..." Dennis paused. "What the fuck kind of sound is that?"

"I don't know," Larry said from right beside Johnnie. A hand wrapped around his throat and it took all his restraint to stay still. "Is he...I think he's purring."

"Lions don't purr."

"Well, whatever he's doing, he's alive," Larry said quietly, but excitedly. "You smashed the back of his head in, so I don't know how, but he's alive."

"And so are you. Are you going to apologize for yelling at me now?"

"Hugh can't be too far. Keep your voice down so he doesn't hear us," Larry said, ignoring Dennis's question. He slid his arms under Johnnie's armpits and began dragging him. "Help me get him far enough away from Hugh that he can't hold his power and then we're home free."

"I don't know about this," Dennis said, but he took hold of Johnnie's ankles and lifted him off the ground.

"Now's not the time to second guess our plan. Do you have any idea how much a Premier Pride will pay for a young Siphon? And with your asshole Premier gone, we'll be able to run the Berk pride."

"He isn't an asshole," Dennis muttered.

"Whatever. Doesn't matter anymore. As soon as we get the Siphon far enough from him, he'll be dead." Larry's breath was labored and his hold on Johnnie slipped. "He's heavier than he looks."

He was also healthier than he looked. In fact, he was almost completely healed. Whatever damage Dennis had done to Johnnie's head must have repaired itself from the purring, same with the lacerations made by Larry. So now Johnnie just had to figure out how to escape from two deranged lions before they got him too far from Hugh. If it had been one on one, he was sure he could have done it, but with both of them against him, he had to be cautious.

"He stopped," Dennis said.

"Huh?"

"The noise he was making." Dennis fumbled with his hold and almost dropped Johnnie's feet. "The purring, or whatever, he stopped."

"Dennis! Focus." Larry grunted as he tried to keep a firm grasp on Johnnie's upper body. "Hugh can't be far. This has taken too long already. We need to move faster."

"I think this was a mistake."

"Damn it! You're the one who said the Premier was weak."

"I didn't say he was weak. I said he was vulnerable because the Siphon almost killed him."

"Same difference." Larry growled. "We talked about this. If the Premier can die just from the Siphon jumping off a dresser, he's at risk anyway. What good will it do for the pride if he dies and there's nobody there to take over? And if the Siphon is defective, wouldn't it be better if we sold him? That way we get rid of the problem, earn enough money to last us our whole lives, and have the Berk pride under our control."

Larry's explanation made Johnnie realize how much damage he had caused with his suicide attempt. Lions who knew about it could perceive Hugh as vulnerable, which in turn made him vulnerable and put his life at risk. And if Hugh died, the entire pride would be at the mercy of whoever managed to step in. Of course, if Johnnie had succeeded in ending his own life, Hugh would have died too and the pride would have been left in the same predicament. None of that was hard to figure out, but Johnnie hadn't realized it because he'd been thinking only about finding freedom from the pain of spending every day being utterly and completely ignored by everyone, including the person who was a part of him.

"We're not going to control Berk," Dennis corrected. "We can *lead* the pride."

"That's what I said."

"No, it isn't."

Dennis let go of Johnnie's legs and walked away. Larry followed him, dragging Johnnie along.

"It's the same thing. With Hugh Langley gone, the two of us teaming up, and the money from the Siphon in our pockets, the Berk pride will be ours."

"The money will belong to the pride," Dennis said. "We can't keep it for ourselves."

"That money is going to be *ours*," Larry responded angrily. He released his hold on Johnnie, letting him slide to the ground, and stomped away in the direction of Dennis's voice, which sounded to be at least a dozen feet in front of them.

"How do you figure?" Dennis asked.

"We're the ones who earned it."

"Earned it? By doing what?"

"Coming up with this plan! Implementing it! Seeing it through!"

"That doesn't make any sense," Dennis said tiredly. "Look, I agreed to this because I thought it'd help the pride, but it won't. We need to stop before it's too late."

"It's already too late!"

It wasn't too late, but it would be if Dennis and Larry stopped arguing and moved Johnnie enough distance from

Hugh to snap their connection. Considering how far he had been to begin with and how long they'd been walking, Johnnie was surprised not to sense any disruption in his ability to carry Hugh's power.

Knowing he wasn't likely to get a better chance at escape than he had at that moment with the two men bickering, Johnnie opened his eyes just enough to see his surroundings. He had hoped to be able to figure out what direction to run in to get back to Hugh, but without being able to raise his head or do more than squint, from his vantage point on the ground, the landscape looked the same in all directions.

Johnnie's best bet would be to pop up, run in the opposite direction from Dennis and Larry, and get a better look at the sky to find the setting sun. Then he could head north, where Hugh was watching the elk. But if he ran in his human form, Larry and Dennis would shift into their lions and catch him almost immediately. That meant he had to shift before he could get away and because he wasn't as powerful as Hugh, his shift would take time and likely get the other lions' attention.

Much as he wanted to avoid that problem, he had no choice but to shift as quietly as possible and hope that Larry and Dennis wouldn't notice soon enough to knock him out again. His decision made, Johnnie put all his focus into shifting into his beast. He heard shouts, felt the thud of sticks and rocks, but either he'd had enough lead time to avoid a more thorough attack or Larry and Dennis hadn't aimed well because before long, he was on four feet, dashing through the brush, the minor injuries he'd sustained during his escape healing as quickly as his pace.

Though Larry and Dennis had managed to transport him a fair distance, as a lion running at full speed, Johnnie made it up in no time, so he soon found himself in the spot where he had been captured. He was about to double back the way he had originally come so he could get to Hugh when a furious roar, loud enough to be heard for miles, shook the trees and ground. Unlike the reaction he'd had to being attacked by Larry, this sound had Johnnie willingly rolling over and showing his vulnerable belly.

Within seconds, Hugh's massive black lion towered over him. He sniffed at Johnnie's fur, lapped at the drying blood, and chuffed disapprovingly. After he'd examined every area where Johnnie had been wounded, he straddled Johnnie's smaller frame and licked his neck and face.

Despite the danger he had just escaped and the possibility that it wasn't over, Hugh's affectionate grooming and tender attention aroused Johnnie. He whimpered and fidgeted, his breath speeding up and his dick hardening. It was all he could do to remember that Larry and Dennis were still out there, which meant Hugh's safety was at risk. Johnnie closed his eyes, blocking out the sight of the gorgeous black lion, and focused on changing into his human skin.

By the time he opened his human eyes, Hugh's hands were mapping his chest and flank.

"There's a lot of blood but no marks." Hugh looked up

from Johnnie's torso and met his gaze. "The blood is yours. I tasted it."

"I healed."

Dipping his chin, Hugh said, "I figured." His nostrils flared, eyes narrowed, and voice deepened. "Who hurt you?"

"Larry Ridley." Still lying on his back, Johnnie scrambled to sit up. "Dennis Jones was with him. He was part of it, but I think he ended up regretting that."

"Where're you going?" Hugh wrapped his hand around Johnnie's throat, holding him in place but not hurting him.

"They're still out there and they want to kill you." Johnnie tried to stay calm, but just thinking about Larry Ridley's plan to destroy Hugh had him panicking. "We need to catch them before they escape and try this again when we're not looking."

Incredibly, Hugh threw his head back and laughed.

"I'm serious. They're dangerous. Or at least Larry is. I'm not sure about Dennis."

"What they are is dead." Hugh curled his hand around Johnnie's nape and traced his jaw with his thumb. "They hurt you," he rasped. "Dead men walking. Both of them."

"They didn't mean to. That's what I'm trying to tell you." Johnnie breathed in deeply, getting calm enough to make sense. "It was all a ploy to get to you. They wanted to separate us enough to break our connection so you'd die. Then they'd take over Berk, sell me to another pride, and pocket the money."

"They planned to *sell* you?" Hugh growled.

"Larry did. Well, Dennis too, but he said the money would be for the pride. That's when they argued and—"

"*Sell* you?" Hugh said, again, his voice quieter but much scarier. "You are not property to be sold."

That comment left Johnnie momentarily speechless. "I'm a Siphon." He blinked rapidly. "Prides sell Siphons to other prides or give them to Premiers in exchange for leading their pride."

Hugh's expression went from furious to sickened to sad. "You are not for sale."

They were going in circles. "The money wasn't the driving factor. It was about taking over Berk. That's what I'm trying to tell you. They want to kill you so they can take over the pride." Johnnie jerked his head from side to side and squinted, trying to see if Larry and Dennis were hiding, waiting to attack again. "And they're still out here."

Keeping his arm around Johnnie's waist, Hugh rose. "We need to get you home and clean you up."

It was as if they were having two different conversations. "Do you hear what I'm telling you? Maybe if we go now, together, we can catch them. I think we were in"—Johnnie glanced around—"that direction." He looked at the disrupted brush littering the ground and nodded. "Yes. That's where they took me." Another thought distracted him from his own point and he looked at Hugh. "When did you get here?"

Hugh drew his eyebrows together and, looking concerned, nudged Johnnie's shoulder until he turned around. "They hit your head." Air-soft fingers skittered over his hair. "You're coated in dried blood." He turned Johnnie back around. "This looks like it was bad. Are you sure you're healed?"

"Uh-huh. I purred and healed, just like always. So when did you get here?"

"Johnnie, I was always here." Hugh cupped both of his cheeks and tilted his head up so their eyes met. "Do you remember that we came to hunt together? We were trying your great new hunting idea."

His brain was working just fine, but if Hugh kept touching him so tenderly, looking at him with so much focus, and saying his name so sweetly, his heart and his groin would explode.

"Yes, I remember. I'm fine, I promise." Johnnie gripped Hugh's wrists. "This spot here is about the farthest distance I was going to get from you on my way to the southern side of the clearing, right? I had to go west to get around the stream and then I'd double back to the east and end up directly south of where you were."

"Right." Hugh rubbed his thumbs under Johnnie's chin and across his neck. "You remember." He sounded relieved.

"Uh-huh. They took me from here and went even farther west." Johnnie flicked his gaze in the direction Larry and Dennis had carried him. "Were you still in the original spot, watching for me to get to the south? Because that distance has to be farther than we got at the festival." Johnnie mentally calculated the size of the festival grounds and how long it had taken him to return from where he'd been snatched, running at full speed in his lion skin. "Much farther."

"I got here at the same time as you," Hugh said. He slid his fingers over Johnnie's temples, massaging. "I waited for you to get to the other side of the herd, but it was taking too long so I knew something was wrong. I came after you and that's when I saw you running over, coated in blood."

"We've never been able to be more than one room apart if the doors were closed and we couldn't see each other," Johnnie pointed out. "First the festival and now this. It's so much farther and, Hugh—" Johnnie licked his lips and looked into Hugh's eyes. "I didn't feel any strain on our connection."

"I didn't either."

"Why?" Thought after thought bounced in Johnnie's head as he tried to make sense of the change. Siphons were so rare that he had never met another one, but he'd heard every detail about what was expected of him. He knew he had to stay connected to Hugh at all times and his experience had confirmed that limitation. Whenever he had gotten too far from Hugh and couldn't see him, the path between them had instantly frayed, and they'd had to see each other or get closer together to make sure it didn't snap and endanger Hugh by releasing too much power into his body.

"Stop thinking so hard. We'll figure it out, but right now, we need to get you home." Hugh rubbed one huge palm over Johnnie's bare chest. "You were hurt. From the blood on your body and hair, it was bad." Hugh's lips were tight, his forehead wrinkled, and his eyes pained. "If you didn't have that healing purr they would have killed you." He shook his head and cleared his throat. "You're bloody and dirty and I need to clean you up and look at you under the light to make sure nothing's wrong."

"If we don't go after Larry now, he'll get away. Dennis too." It was probably too late already. The fact that they hadn't attacked again, meant they realized they couldn't beat Hugh so they'd retreated. But Johnnie had heard the determination in Larry's voice and knew he wouldn't stop. "They'll come after you again. We need to catch them."

"Don't worry about them. They're just a couple of greedy, selfish lions." Hugh ghosted his fingers over the back of Johnnie's head, where he had been wounded. "They attacked you, injured you, and planned to sell you. If they're dumb enough to stay on my pride lands, I'll find them and kill them. If they're dumb enough to go near any other pride lands, including Larry's pride, I'll get word out and they'll be held until I can get to them and kill them. And if they're dumb enough to go rogue and live on their own, the lack of a pride and resources will kill them." Hugh swiped his thumb over Johnnie's lower lip. "Any way you slice it, same result. Dead men walking."

CHAPTER 12

"I'LL go shower," Johnnie said as soon as they walked into the bedroom.

He turned toward the doorway to his room when Hugh skated his palm down his back and then grasped his hip, stopping him.

"My shower's bigger." Hugh curled his arm around Johnnie's waist and led him toward the bathroom.

Knowing Hugh was worried about him warmed Johnnie, but he was fine. And even if he wasn't, he didn't see how using Hugh's shower instead of his own would help.

"I'm smaller than you. I don't need all that space," Johnnie pointed out. Hugh was seven feet tall and weighed three hundred pounds. Everyone was smaller than him. "Besides, you need to wash up too." Hugh wasn't covered in dried blood, but he'd been in the dirt with Johnnie and both of them had built up a sweat running and shifting.

"That's why we need to use my shower." Hugh continued walking as he spoke, leading them through the doorway into his spacious bathroom. "We'll have enough room in here to clean up together."

Stumbling over nothing, Johnnie almost fell to the

white marble floor face first. Thankfully, Hugh still gripped his waist so he kept him upright.

"I knew losing all that blood impacted you." Hugh rubbed his hands over Johnnie's shoulders and looked in his eyes. "I shouldn't have let you run home. I should have carried you."

"You wanted to carry me?"

"You're dizzy," Hugh explained.

It sure felt like it at that moment. "You want me to shower with you?"

"The tile's hard. You could fall in there. I need to—" Hugh swallowed. "Is that a problem?"

Fantasy was the word Johnnie would have used. "No. Not a problem," he said, his heart racing and lungs working overtime.

"The hot water and steam aren't a good idea if you're light-headed." Hugh's forehead crinkled and he tightened his grip on Johnnie. "Maybe we should skip the shower."

"I'm not light-headed," Johnnie assured him, desperately wanting to step under the spray with Hugh.

"Are you sure? Because you sound like you're having trouble breathing and your face looks pale."

Torn between embarrassing himself by explaining his body's reaction or destroying the opportunity to get wet and slippery with a naked Hugh, Johnnie chose the option most likely to get him access to Hugh's hard cock.

"I'm aroused," he confessed as he dropped his gaze to his own dick, which was fully erect and parallel to his stomach. "Really, really aroused."

Following Johnnie's line of sight, Hugh's chest rumbled. "Johnnie?" Hugh slid one hand behind Johnnie's neck and the other down his chest. "Tell me what it feels like."

"What it feels like?" Johnnie repeated.

"Yes." Hugh dipped his chin. "Arousal." He looked at Johnnie's erection and then back at his face. "Tell me what it feels like to be aroused."

Was it a test? Did Hugh want to make sure Johnnie was telling the truth about not being damaged by Larry and Dennis's attack?

"Um. Well, I get this feeling in my stomach"—he put his palm on his lower belly, next to the base of his cock—"right here. It's like a pull or a rush, like heat."

Hugh moved his fingertips around Johnnie's hand. "Here?"

"Ungh… Uh-huh. And my heart beats faster, which then makes me breathe faster like you said."

Hugh brushed his hand across Johnnie's chest, making his nipples pebble.

"And my skin's more sensitive everywhere, but especially there."

"Here?" Hugh traced Johnnie's nipple.

Whimpering, Johnnie nodded.

"Does it hurt?"

"No," Johnnie said breathlessly as he squirmed under Hugh's attention. "Aches a little, but in a good way."

Taking Johnnie's nipple between his thumb and

forefinger, Hugh pinched and rolled the wrinkled nub. "Do you know that I never felt that?"

"What...what do you mean?"

"All these years, getting off hasn't been like that for me."

"What was it like?"

Tilting his head to the side and letting out a deep breath, Hugh seemed to consider the question.

"You know how when you're so hungry your stomach hurts and then you eat and it feels better? It's a relief, but it isn't pleasurable." While still playing with Johnnie's nipples, Hugh moved him closer to the wall, leaned him against it, and then, once Johnnie was stable, dropped his free hand to Johnnie's cock. "That's what sex was like."

"Oh Lord," Johnnie moaned. Drops of liquid slid from his slit down his shaft and Hugh rubbed his palm over them. "I can't...can't think when you do that."

"You don't need to think."

"I want—" He moaned. "Want to understand what you're saying."

"With you, it isn't that type of hunger."

"It's not?" Johnnie squeaked.

"No." Hugh shook his head. "With you it's like eating a perfect piece of steak." He leaned down and breathed across Johnnie's jaw over to his ear. "You smell it and your mouth waters with desire." He circled his fingers around Johnnie's shaft. "You close your eyes because it's all you want to focus on." He moved his hand up and down slowly. "You bite into it, the juices seep out, and it tastes like nothing else." He suckled Johnnie's earlobe. "You don't want the experience to end." He played with each of his nipples in turn. "Doesn't matter if your stomach's empty or not because you're ravenous for the flavor. And when you're so full that you have to stop, you regret it because you want more." He rubbed his thumb over Johnnie's crown, flicked his tongue across his ear, and pinched his nipple. "You always want more."

"Hugh!" Johnnie cried out. He clutched Hugh's chest, arched his back, and went on tiptoe. "Oh, Lord, Hugh!" One more moan and then Johnnie stopped breathing, stopped seeing, and did nothing but feel white-hot joy course through him as his balls emptied and he pulsed ejaculate over Hugh's fingers and across his torso.

When he could finally open his eyes, he saw Hugh raise his slick hand to his own mouth. With his dark gaze glued to Johnnie's, he licked his palm and then moaned. "That's what I mean." Hugh licked again. "Delicious."

His body boneless and his brain hazy with satisfaction, Johnnie walked into the shower in a fog. He went through the steps of bathing by rote, unaware of anything other than the man with him. The water glistened on Hugh's massive frame, highlighting it, and Johnnie wanted to lick him all over. He settled for dropping to his knees and burying his face in

Hugh's balls.

"You smell so good." He inhaled again, smelling Hugh beneath the soap, and groaned. "So good." He turned his head from side to side, rubbing Hugh's scent over his face. "I hated smelling them on you."

After a pause, Hugh said, "I scent the pride everywhere, but I didn't know my body smelled like them after we fucked."

"It did," Johnnie croaked, the memory of other lions' odors on Hugh sickening him. He parted his lips and sucked one large nut into his mouth, moaning at the rightness of Hugh's flavor and letting it wash away the tainted memories. "They're gone now."

"You're so sensitive." Hugh slid one finger around the perimeter of Johnnie's ear. "All of your senses." He moved his fingertip down Johnnie's nose. "You can smell things even when the scent's too old for me to track." He traced Johnnie's eyebrow. "It's why the seams on your clothes bother you, why you get so cold."

Unsure how to respond, Johnnie shrugged. "I only know I smelled them before and now I don't." He licked a swipe up Hugh's testicles. "Now you just smell like you."

"And you," Hugh rumbled.

While still worshiping Hugh's testicles, Johnnie looked up questioningly.

"I do." Hugh stroked his big hand over Johnnie's hair. "I've noticed it." He met Johnnie's gaze, his expression serious. "The pride and its members are background for me, constantly there but not something I distinguish or notice.

You—" He shuddered. "I can smell you on me all the time."

Was that a bad thing? Johnnie tried to read Hugh's expression.

"It makes me hard," Hugh said reassuringly.

The reminder had Johnnie sliding his cheek back and forth over Hugh's rigid cock. "You're so hot and smooth." He traced a prominent vein with his lips. "Is this really because of me?"

"Yes." Hugh gripped his cock with one hand and Johnnie's chin with the other, and then, holding Johnnie's face in place, he painted his lips with his glans. "It's different with you, the way I feel."

"Why?" Johnnie asked, unable to finish his actual questions: *Why didn't you notice me before? What's different now?*

As if he could hear Johnnie's thoughts, or maybe he'd been wondering the same thing, Hugh answered the unspoken questions. "When we met, I had my own pride to take care of plus the new members from Westgate to integrate. Some of them were sick and weak. They didn't all get along, especially the males. We needed to build more homes, find them jobs." Hugh sighed. "You were the Siphon. You could carry my power, finally lift that burden, so I didn't have that to think about, and I..." He swallowed hard and tilted his head back, letting the shower spray trickle over his face. "I never looked for more." He blinked the water out of his eyes, peered down at Johnnie, and cupped both his cheeks. "I never looked at you."

As beautiful as Hugh's eyes were, as intelligent and insightful, for years, they'd chilled Johnnie to his core because they'd never landed on him.

"But now?" Johnnie asked.

Turning his lips up, Hugh said, "Now that I know you, I see you." He chuckled and shook his head, not tearing his gaze away. "Now I have trouble seeing anything but you."

Though a part of him wanted to ask more questions just so Hugh would keep saying kind things to him, more of him was overwhelmed by a need to join with Hugh in as many ways as possible. With Hugh's erection directly in front of his face, Johnnie knew where to start. He darted his tongue out for a small taste and, immediately needing more, opened his mouth and dropped it over the rigid length.

"Johnnie," Hugh said breathlessly, reverently. "Yes."

Praise about making Hugh feel good fulfilled Johnnie as much as his compliments. He moaned happily and stayed on task, licking, sucking, and bobbing on Hugh's cock while he fondled his balls. Remembering Hugh saying blow jobs weren't normally enough to bring him to satisfaction, Johnnie felt proud when precum dripped steadily onto his tongue. He could give Hugh something the others couldn't, which made him important to the person who had been the center of his world for a decade.

From the first moment Hugh's power had entered Johnnie's body, bringing Hugh inside him at the most fundamental level and giving him unique insight into the Premier's protective, generous, intelligent spirit, Johnnie had lived in awe of him, constantly longing for more ties, more connections, more forms of closeness. And now he had all those things and more. Hugh sought his opinions about matters important to the pride and chatted with him about even the most trivial things that occupied his mind. Hugh slept with him every night and didn't merely share his bed; he held him close, his arms and sometimes even a leg wrapped around Johnnie. And Hugh kissed him, stroked him, and caressed him, making him soar. Johnnie wanted—*needed*—to matter to Hugh in the same way Hugh mattered to him, to be someone Hugh enjoyed instead of tolerated, maybe even someone Hugh longed for, the way he longed for Hugh.

"Do you want it in your mouth?" Hugh wiped his thumb across Johnnie's spit-slick chin.

His dick throbbing, his nuts tightening, and his mouth watering, Johnnie could only whimper and suck harder. The day's earlier stresses and worries faded away to nothing until Johnnie's only focus was Hugh's scent, Hugh's flavor, Hugh's pleasure.

"Don't know how you do this to me, but I'm almost there. Damn, you're so good." Hugh tenderly brushed his fingers through Johnnie's hair, the softness of the gesture at odds with the size and strength of the man.

When Hugh continued petting his hair and also began grunting and thrusting his hips, Johnnie clutched his thighs but otherwise completely let go. He followed Hugh's pace and flowed with his every motion.

"Here it comes, Johnnie," Hugh said. "All for you." His grip tightened in Johnnie's hair, his breath hitched, his legs went stick-straight, and then warm, tangy ejaculate pulsed onto Johnnie's tongue and down his throat, bringing yet another part of Hugh into him and raising his arousal to an almost pained fever pitch. "Only for you."

With those words, pleasure tingled from the top of Johnnie's head down to his toes and satisfaction washed over him, equal in its intensity to any orgasm he'd had with Hugh, but instead of heating his groin, it burned into his heart, warming him from the inside out. He rested his forehead against Hugh's hip, his heart racing, his lungs heaving, and his cock dripping.

"Let's get you in bed."

Johnnie opened his eyes and realized he was out of the shower, being held in Hugh's muscular arms, a towel draped around him.

"You're exhausted." Hugh kissed his forehead and began walking out of the bathroom. "Your body needs rest to heal."

"I'm fine," Johnnie insisted, because he truly was. He felt no aftereffects from Larry's attack, and he wasn't tired, at least not in the way Hugh meant.

"You were so zoned out in the shower, you didn't know I was lifting you, and you can barely keep your eyes open now."

"I'm relaxed." Johnnie sighed contentedly and rested his cheek against Hugh's shoulder. "Really relaxed."

"Are you hungry?" Hugh tugged the blanket back, lay Johnnie on the bed, and then covered him up to his neck. "We missed dinner."

The reminder caused some of Johnnie's earlier worries to resurface. "I'm okay." Johnnie reached for Hugh's hand, not wanting him to leave. "But we need to talk about earlier."

"Everything's going to be fine."

Apparently, Johnnie looked as convinced as he felt, because Hugh sighed, dropped the towel he held, and then climbed into bed.

"They're two not particularly strong, not particularly big, not particularly fast, and, it's now clear, not particularly smart lions. Even when I was their age, I could have easily defeated the two of them in a fight. Now I've got seventy years on them." He shook his head and snorted. "Labeling what I'm going to do to them a fight is a mockery to fights everywhere. You have nothing to worry about."

That was true if Hugh went head-to-head with Larry and Dennis. "But what if they don't fight with you?" Johnnie pointed out. "They must realize that's not a winning strategy, which is why they didn't take that approach today." He looked away regretfully. "They know I'm your vulnerability so they caught me and ran. They tried to break our connection to destroy you."

"They tried and they failed."

"That's just it." Johnnie sat up, too worked-up to stay still. "They didn't fail."

Hugh looked down at himself, and then back at Johnnie,

and arched his eyebrows.

"They didn't destroy you," Johnnie agreed. "But they took me far enough that our connection should have snapped." Johnnie knit his eyebrows together and chewed his bottom lip. "I still don't understand why it didn't."

"You'll figure it out."

He would? Did Hugh know something he didn't? "How? Do you know why we were able to get so far apart?"

"No, but you're the smart one in this operation." Hugh winked and got up. "I'm sure you'll come up with an explanation."

Worried that Hugh took their ability to separate as permission to free himself from Johnnie's constant presence, Johnnie barely registered the compliment. "Where're you going?" he asked breathlessly.

"You went from drowsy to jittery in less than a minute." Hugh walked to the closet and came back with a sweatshirt and socks, which he handed to Johnnie. "Your blood sugar's low. We need to get food into you."

"My blood sugar's fine."

Hugh curled his palm around the side of Johnnie's face. "Put those on and we'll go downstairs."

Unable to resist anything in the wake of Hugh's touch, Johnnie slipped the clothes on. "I know you're worried but I'm completely healed," he said.

"Humor me," Hugh said as he reached his hand out.

Immediately, Johnnie took his hand, as usual, warming at any offer to connect with his powerful Premier.

Connect.

Johnnie froze in place and gasped loudly.

"What?" Hugh immediately darted his gaze around the room, searching for threats.

"Nothing," Johnnie said, even though it wasn't nothing. It was an explanation. He shook his head and concentrated on moving his muscles. "Sorry."

Before he could share his theory, he needed to think it through, turn it over in his mind, and figure out if it made sense. His stomach rumbled noisily. But first he needed to eat.

"Not hungry?" Hugh said, looking at him knowingly.

"Maybe a little." The rumble turned into a loud growl. "Maybe more than a little." Johnnie smiled ruefully.

Grinning back at him, Hugh said, "Let's go see what we can throw together." Still holding Johnnie's hand, he walked toward the door.

Trusting in Hugh to lead, Johnnie followed along without looking where he was going, his attention, instead, captivated by Hugh's fingers curled with his. *Connected.*

CHAPTER 13

"PREMER?" Percy Milroy said as he knocked on Hugh's office door. "Do you have a minute?"

"Sure." Hugh shook hands with the man and woman in his office and kissed their cheeks before saying goodbye. "Come on in."

The day had been a whirlwind. Hugh wanted to warn every pride member about the danger posed by Dennis Jones and his friend Larry, both because he needed his lions to stay safe and because he needed to be notified if either man made contact. Without a pride gathering scheduled, he had two choices—demand that everyone drop whatever they had planned to come to an impromptu meeting or spend his day going from pride home to pride home, sharing the information in small groups. Johnnie wasn't surprised when Hugh said he didn't want to create panic and upheaval, and instead of disrupting everyone's schedule, he'd spend the day visiting members in their pride homes.

Though the current configuration of his relationship with Hugh was only a month old, Johnnie had carried part of his Premier inside for a decade so he had long known that Hugh was a good man who would put his pride members before himself. Any lions who weren't home during his individual visits had been invited to Hugh's house that evening, where he had shared the information once again and had then made himself available to answer questions.

"What can I do for you, Percy?" Hugh asked once the latest grouping of lions left and Percy stepped inside the office door.

"I, uh—" Percy gulped and flicked his gaze toward Johnnie, who was sitting in his usual spot, an upholstered chair in the corner. "I mean, *we* wanted to run something by you." He walked farther into the office, followed by a couple of other lions.

"Sure. Take a seat." Hugh smiled tiredly and pointed toward the chairs gathered around his desk. It was almost ten at night and they had started making the rounds from pride home to pride home at eight that morning. Hugh had to be exhausted.

The lions shuffled in, sat down, and fidgeted. Most of the pride had trusted in Hugh's assurance that he'd deal with Dennis and Larry and they had nothing to worry about. A small number had been visibly furious that one of their own had betrayed the pride, and they'd offered to assist Hugh in any retribution he chose to inflict. A scant few had been nervous. But none of the lions had displayed the anxiety evident from those who now sat in Hugh's office, picking at their clothes and avoiding Hugh's gaze.

"Could we..." Percy glanced at Johnnie, took a deep breath, and then looked at Hugh and said, "Can we speak alone?" He wiped his hands on his jeans and shuffled in his seat. "The Siphon can wait outside the door and not be too far to hold your power, right?"

Narrowing his eyes, Hugh said, "Why do you want to separate me from my Siphon?"

"I don't!" Percy said, sounding panicked. "This is sensitive and... Please, Premier."

After looking at Percy appraisingly, Hugh turned to Johnnie, and though he didn't say anything, Johnnie knew Hugh wanted to grant Percy's request.

For years Johnnie had thought that if Hugh hadn't been such a good man, his own life would have been easier. He might have been able to tolerate his duties as a Siphon if only he hadn't been tortured by the denial of what he wanted most of all—to be noticed by the generous, selfless, intelligent Premier whose power coursed through him. Those days were behind him, though. He now had Hugh's attention and affection, so he had no hesitation about giving other lions alone time with their Premier in the midst of a stressful situation.

Nodding quietly, Johnnie got up, stepped out of the office, and shut the door behind him. Muffled conversations from pride members chatting in the front room wafted over. Not wanting to interrupt them, he remained in the hallway. Almost immediately, he realized that his close proximity to Hugh's office and his sensitive hearing allowed him to make out the conversation inside.

"What's going on, Percy?" Hugh asked. "You look like

you're about to shake apart."

After a long pause, one of the other lions—Van Hartwick, a pride elder—said, "He's nervous, Premier." He cleared his throat. "We're all nervous."

"Don't be. I will handle the situation with Dennis Jones and Larry Ridley. The only thing I need from you is to notify me immediately if either of them make contact and to keep your distance from them until I arrive." The instructions were identical to what Hugh had said to every group of lions he'd spoken to that day.

"But what if *they* aren't the danger?" asked Lorena Mansfield.

"I realize this is difficult for all of us," Hugh said patiently. "Dennis was our friend and a valued member of this pride. But unfortunately, he decided to put his own greed above the welfare of the pride and that is dangerous."

"How do you know that's what happened?" asked Lorena. "When you recounted the story, you said you never saw Dennis or his friend. You said the Siphon told you he'd been taken."

The silence that followed the question was filled with so much tension, Johnnie squirmed from his post in the hallway.

"What are you suggesting?" Hugh's tone was perfectly level.

"Premier, I don't know how else to say this but... Have you considered the possibility that the Siphon is lying?" Lorena asked.

"Johnnie doesn't lie to me." There wasn't an ounce of doubt in Hugh's voice, making Johnnie's chest swell.

"How can you know?" Percy asked, sounding frantic. "He already tried to kill you once! I was there that night. Lorena was there. You were..." There was a pause before Percy continued speaking, his voice shaking. "He almost succeeded."

The reminder of what he had done and how it reflected on Hugh dimmed the warmth Johnnie had been feeling, leaving his stomach pained.

"Maybe he was running from you, hoping to get far enough to snap your connection and push all your power back into you again. Then when you caught him, he made an excuse," said Lorena. "Doesn't that make more sense than his story?"

"Johnnie wouldn't do that," Hugh insisted.

Normally, that would have been enough to end the conversation and convince the pride members to defer to their Premier, but whether it was the stress of the situation or the result of Johnnie's previous action, they didn't trust quite as easily in their Premier's judgment.

"The Siphon can't get very far from you. That means if Dennis and Larry had taken him, you would have seen them or at least heard or scented them," Percy pointed out.

Johnnie held his breath, hoping they would believe Hugh once he explained that the two of them could now separate for longer distances. But Hugh didn't explain.

"I can see that you're concerned," Hugh said instead. "I

know how close you are with Dennis, and I'm truly sorry he chose this path, Percy."

"That's not why I'm saying this," Percy croaked, but his breaking voice proved that Hugh was right in his assessment, like always. "The Siphon tried to kill you and to make sure he wouldn't do it again, you've had to watch him so closely that you haven't spent yourself with anyone in the pride since that night. I know. I asked around."

"I gather you're probably relieving yourself with him but you need more than one lion to drain all your seed, Premier," said Van.

Bile rose in Johnnie's throat. Was that why Hugh had started touching him? And was it why Hugh had stopped having sex with the rest of the pride members?

"Without more frequent releases, your hormones will build up and you'll be —"

"Violent. Temperamental. Lacking in control." Hugh listed each characteristic in the same slow, calm cadence he'd had throughout the conversation. "Did I miss anything?"

"No," Van said, sounding confused. "That's right."

"Do I look angry, Van?"

There wasn't a verbal response so Johnnie assumed Van had either shaken his head or become too nervous to speak.

"I'm sitting in my office with three trusted members of my pride and they're continuously questioning my judgment and second guessing my decisions." Though the words were harsh, the tone remained even. "Is that something most

Premiers would tolerate, Lorena?"

"No," she answered.

"Have I lost my temper, Percy?"

"No," Percy rasped.

"I'm glad we agree on those points. Let's see if we can get on the same page about the rest of it. Percy, when was the last time you saw Dennis?"

"I, uh… Yesterday. I saw him yesterday morning."

"Did he tell you he'd be traveling away from Berk?"

After a long pause, Percy said, "No."

"He lives in your den. You're the most senior lion there. Isn't it practice for the lions in your den to notify you before they're gone overnight?"

"Yes," Percy confirmed.

"And yet, Dennis didn't tell you he'd be leaving. He didn't tell me either, and I'm his Premier. Though I give this pride a lot of autonomy, a lion can be removed from a pride for leaving pride lands without his Premier's permission."

Nervous mumbles sounded in response to Hugh's point.

"I spoke with George at the service station who confirmed that Dennis was on the schedule today but he didn't show up," Hugh added.

"He missed work?" Lorena asked in surprise. "He never misses work."

"Yes," Hugh said. "At this point, we can all agree on two things—after a century walking this earth, I have the ability to know what my body needs and Dennis Jones broke

protocol by leaving Berk without permission or notification."
When nobody argued, Hugh continued. "Let's add a third
item to the list. Your theory is that Johnnie made up the story
about being attacked by Dennis and Larry because he was
trying to run from me in order to break our connection and
kill me. Is that right?"

"It made more sense than Dennis attacking him and..."
Percy's voice trailed off.

"Right. You believed he was trying to run from me.
And with that thought in mind, the three of you came in
here about"—there was a pause—"seven minutes ago and
asked to speak to me alone." Another pause and the sound
of Hugh's chair rolling over the wood floor. "How far do you
think Johnnie has to get to sever our connection and destroy
me by relinquishing my power?" Footsteps. "And how long do
you think it'd take him to get that far if he shifted into his lion
form and ran?" Gasps sounded along with scrapes, as if chairs
were pushed back in a rush. "Is seven minutes enough?" Hugh
said, his voice remaining as calm as it had been throughout
the conversation. "How about eight minutes? Because that's
how long it's been now." The doorknob rattled. "I realize
you were shaken by what Johnnie did that night and that
it makes it difficult for you to trust him, but all you need to
do is trust *me*." The doorknob turned and the door opened
a hair. "Johnnie," Hugh spoke into the crack without looking
out. "Please come in here."

Wiping his sweaty palms on his pants legs, Johnnie
took a calming breath, stepped toward the door, and pulled

it open the remainder of the way. Immediately in front of the door stood Hugh. The other three lions were gathered behind him next to the chairs they had previously occupied, their faces pale and mouths gaping, as if in shock.

"Van, Lorena, Percy." Hugh looked at them. "Are we done or do you want to continue our conversation?"

Flicking his gaze between Hugh and Johnnie, Van said, "We're done, Premier." He walked over to Hugh and lowered his gaze respectfully. "Thank you for your time."

"You're welcome, Van." Hugh caressed his shoulder. "Good night."

Van walked out of the office and Lorena approached Hugh.

"My apologies," she whispered, her eyes lowered and her face red.

Hugh kissed her cheek. "My best to your little ones, Lorena."

"Thank you." She sniffled and then rushed out of the room.

"Hugh, I…" Percy gulped and blinked rapidly.

"Come here." Hugh opened his arms and Percy rushed over.

He clung to Hugh, hiding his face against Hugh's chest as his body shook.

"It's that friend of his," Percy said, his words muffled but still understandable. "He kept causing trouble. Dennis never would have done this on his own. He loves Berk and he worships you." He shook his head. "I should have made

Larry leave. Then none of this would have happened."

"Dennis is an adult. You're the head of his pride home, but he's not a cub subject to his mother's rules. His choices aren't your responsibility."

"I know." Percy straightened and wiped at his eyes with the backs of his hands. "But he's my closest friend." He sighed. "*Was* my closest friend. I wish I'd noticed what he was getting into in time to stop him before it got too far."

"So do I." Hugh rubbed Percy's back.

Nodding, Percy smiled at Hugh weakly. "Thank you for your patience, Premier. I know I don't deserve it. Good night." He stepped toward the door and then stopped and turned to Johnnie. "Good night, uh, Johnnie."

Surprised at being noticed by a pride member let alone addressed by his new name, it took Johnnie several seconds to respond but eventually he said, "Good night, Percy."

With a nod, Percy turned around and shuffled away, his shoulders slumped.

Hugh remained still, watching the shifters walk out of the room and down the hallway. When their footsteps faded, he sighed deeply and relaxed his shoulders.

"Long day." He moved closer to Johnnie, stood in front of him, and rubbed his shoulders. "How are you holding up? You must be exhausted."

They'd been going from pride home to pride home since morning, constantly surrounded by people and noise, so Johnnie was tired, but the conversation he had overheard bothered him more than the lack of rest. Why hadn't Hugh explained to the pride that they could now separate for a longer distance? Hearing that would have made the situation more understandable. Unless what Percy, Lorena, and Van implied was true. If Hugh insisted on staying close to Johnnie in order to prevent him from making another attempt on his own life, then their ability to separate farther wouldn't matter.

"I'm okay," he said, turning the past month over in his mind. Was it possible he had been seeing what he wanted to see rather than what was actually taking place? Even now, as Hugh massaged him, was he seeing tenderness when in fact there was nothing but obligation?

Hugh had been leading a pride and taking care of its members for longer than most lifetimes. Knowing him as well as he did meant Johnnie realized there was nothing the Premier wouldn't do for his lions. Spending extra time with a person who could harm the pride was by no means outside the limits of Hugh's devotion.

During his conversation with Percy and the other lions, Hugh had essentially denied that was the reason he'd been spending time with Johnnie. But Johnnie now understood how very important it was for the pride to see their Premier as all-powerful, and he recognized the immense impact of any action that took away from that perception. So even if Hugh had chosen to remain close to Johnnie out of self-preservation, he wouldn't have admitted it to the pride members for fear of showing weakness.

There was only one way to know Hugh's reason for

being uncharacteristically close to him—Johnnie would have to ask Hugh. But before he could pose the question, he needed to be prepared for whatever response he received. Because regardless of what had driven Hugh's recent behavior, being close to the Premier and more involved with the pride had brought Johnnie's role in Berk and his importance to the pride to the forefront of his mind. He wouldn't take an action that would hurt the pride, not even if it was his only route to freedom.

"Johnnie?" Hugh slid his hands to either side of Johnnie's neck and caressed the skin behind his ear. "You look"—Hugh peered at Johnnie's face, his brow crinkled in concentration—"drained." He hunched down and brushed his lips over Johnnie's. "Give me a few minutes to make sure everyone's gone and lock up the house. Then we can go to bed." He wrapped his arm around Johnnie and led him out of the office. "I shouldn't have pushed you so hard today. You're still recovering from your injuries."

"I really am okay." Physically, he was fine and he wouldn't make Hugh feel guilty about doing right by the pride. "It was important to meet with everyone."

"It was," Hugh agreed. "But now that's done and we can get some rest."

Johnnie nodded though he doubted he could sleep well that night. He had a lot of thinking to do.

CHAPTER 14

Like he had the previous day, Hugh led Johnnie into his bathroom. His touch gentle and slow, he undressed both of them before curling his arm around Johnnie and keeping him close as they stepped under the spray. As Hugh washed him, Johnnie remained silent and passive, his mind racing, turning over details of how Hugh had been behaving with him, what Percy, Van, and Lorena said, what Dennis did and Larry's role in it, and the change in how far he and Hugh could separate. Endless memories bounced in his head, crossing over each other and distracting him with new information before he could fully digest any single point.

After cleaning Johnnie, Hugh began soaping himself. As he raised his hands to his head and rinsed off his shampoo, his biceps and forearms stretched and bulged and his chest and stomach rippled with lines of muscles. All lions were strong, but nobody compared to Hugh's thick, corded physique. Staring at Hugh's body, Johnnie remembered Hugh asking what turned him on sexually. Johnnie had given him a true, albeit simple answer—Hugh. He could tell that Hugh didn't understand his answer, that he had expected a list of sexual acts or positions, but the fact of the matter was, to

Johnnie, arousal and attraction were irrevocably intertwined with the man standing before him.

When Hugh told him he had experienced pleasure with him, Johnnie believed his feelings were returned, but now he couldn't stop worrying that his own wishes were causing him to misinterpret reality. Without conscious permission, his mouth opened and his concerns tumbled out.

"I overheard you earlier. When you were in your office."

Hugh stepped away from the shower spray and rubbed his palms over his eyes, wiping away the water.

"I didn't mean to eavesdrop but I couldn't *not* hear." Johnnie gulped and fidgeted. "I could have walked farther away, I guess, but then I wouldn't be there if you needed me fast and there were still so many lions in the house and—"

"I have no secrets from you." Hugh cupped both sides of Johnnie's face and tilted it up. "You're *my* Siphon." His dark gaze bored into Johnnie as he slowly inched his thumbs from side to side. "You're the only one who sees and knows everything." Rather than looking resentful or worried about the statement, Hugh's lips turned up at the edges and his eyes softened. "And I'm not surprised your hearing is sensitive, like your other senses." He leaned down and brushed his lips over Johnnie's. "You're special."

"They said you're spending more time with me to stop me from making an attempt on my life and releasing your power," Johnnie said in a rush. Once the words were out, he took a deep breath and forced himself to keep his eyes raised, meeting Hugh's.

"We've always spent our time together," Hugh pointed out, his brow crinkling.

"Not like this." As he spoke, Johnnie wondered if it was possible that the changes, which were so monumental to him, were mere semantics to Hugh.

"No, not like this," Hugh conceded.

Johnnie sighed, relieved that Hugh at least recognized the difference.

"And you want to know if they're right, is that it?" Hugh asked, his voice low and his expression suddenly tired. "You want to know why things have...changed between us."

"Yes," Johnnie said, even though he had no right to question his Premier's motives. He had no idea what he'd do with Hugh's answer because now that he realized his importance to the safety of the pride, he wouldn't jeopardize them. But regardless, he had to know why Hugh was paying him attention.

"Let's dry off and get in bed," Hugh said as he turned off the water. Johnnie's face must have shown his disappointment at not having the question answered because Hugh traced his lips with his finger and said, "We can talk while we're lying down."

"Okay."

They toweled off, brushed their teeth, and then crawled into Hugh's big bed. Johnnie lay on his side, his legs curled up and his hands pressed together and pillowed under his cheek. Hugh lay on his back and looked up at the ceiling.

"At first I gave you my attention because I needed to

keep an eye on you so you wouldn't do anything to hurt the pride. That's how I saw it—an attempt to hurt the pride by killing me."

Johnnie's chest cracked.

"But that was only the beginning. As soon as I started learning who you are, I understood that you weren't trying to hurt me or the pride. I also realized that I'd never known you." Hugh drew in a deep breath and rolled his head to the side, meeting Johnnie's gaze. "Once I got to know the man who had been by my side for years, I stopped worrying about your actions and thought more about mine." Hugh's face fell and his deep voice turned hoarse. "I mistreated you, Johnnie."

"No." Johnnie shook his head. "You were doing your job."

"Yes, I was." Hugh nodded. "But it didn't have to be either-or. I was so focused on the rest of the pride that I didn't see you. I took you for granted." He reached out and combed his fingers through Johnnie's hair, pushing it off his forehead. "You were so young, so innocent." He caressed Johnnie's cheek. "You needed me and you deserved better than what I gave you."

"So is it guilt?" Johnnie asked. "Remorse?" Because to him, those reasons weren't any better than Hugh spending time with him to keep him from making an attempt on his life.

"Yes, I feel remorse for how I treated you. Yes, I feel guilty for the years you suffered alone." Hugh's dark eyes were full of emotion. "But no, Johnnie, those aren't the reasons you're in my bed right now." He curled his hand around the back of Johnnie's head and leaned forward until their lips met. "That's not why I'm touching you."

"No?" Johnnie's voice cracked on the word and his breath sped up.

Hugh shook his head.

"Then why?"

"I am driven to take care of the pride. It's who I am, what I was born to do. I'm used to it. But this, with you..." He kissed Johnnie's forehead. "I don't know the words to explain it." He lay down on his side, facing Johnnie, and slid his hand up and down Johnnie's arm. "There have always been so many people around me, needing me, so it doesn't make any sense and I never realized it, but—" He took a deep breath and let it out. "It's like I was lonely before but now I'm not. Because of you."

Warmth blossomed in Johnnie's chest and his eyes burned. "So you haven't been draining your seed with me instead of the others just because you feel obligated to supervise me?" Johnnie asked, already knowing the answer from what Hugh had said, but needing to hear one last reassurance.

"I screwed the others for decades out of obligation— my body needed the release to keep my hormones even. Sex with you is nothing like that." Hugh pursed his lips and scrunched his eyebrows together, as if he was struggling to put his thoughts into words. "The physical acts might be the same, but with you, they leave me sated like I've never been and I feel it everywhere, not just in my balls and...somehow it's different."

Having books as his companions day after day had taught Johnnie about a variety of topics. He happily read whatever was available, including stories about relationships and emotions between humans. Though shifters didn't relate to each other like non-shifters, Johnnie thought Hugh was describing something he had read about.

"The humans have a phrase for what you're describing," Johnnie offered quietly, nervously.

"For fucking?"

"Yes." Johnnie nodded and swallowed hard. "And also the feelings you were describing. It's all part of the same thing to them."

"We're not humans," Hugh pointed out. The comment wasn't intended to be derisive. The reality was that shifters had as much in common with their animal counterparts as they did with their human ones, which meant they had some similarities but were fundamentally different creatures. That was why shifters didn't live alongside non-shifter lions or humans.

"I know. But some of the things I read in their books apply to us too."

"Like the game theory concept you used to come up with the hunting idea?"

"Yes."

Nodding in understanding, Hugh said, "What's their theory about sex?"

"It's a phrase, not a theory. And it isn't *all* sex but—" Johnnie licked his lips. "Sometimes, depending on the people involved, the humans call it making love."

"Making love," Hugh repeated.

"Uh-huh. The saying is based on the emotion love."

"Love." Hugh paused, his expression thoughtful. "Like what lionesses feel for their cubs?"

"My sense is the depth of the emotion is the same but it's different when it's between unrelated humans. They write about it with a unique intensity and passion, and when humans who love each other have sex, they call it making love."

"Humans believe fucking creates an emotion more intense than the formation of life?" Hugh asked incredulously. "Why? It's a bodily function."

"I think it's the other way around. They call it making love, but they don't write about it as if the physical act creates the emotion. Instead, the passionate feeling comes first and it's so all-consuming, they need to express it physically, sexually. That's when it's more than a bodily function so they call it making love."

For several minutes, Hugh continued smoothing his hand over Johnnie's skin and gazing at him, but he didn't speak. "And you believe that's what we're doing?" he eventually asked.

"I was empty," Johnnie croaked. He cleared his throat. "Not the part of me that holds your power, you're so strong, you always kept that full. But there was another space, and no matter how much your power grew, it never filled that spot, but now you're there and I'm not empty anymore."

"You believe the reason sex is so different with us is because instead of screwing we're doing what the humans call making love and that fills an empty part of you?"

"No, I..." Johnnie shook his head and closed his eyes. "I love you, Hugh." He forced himself to be brave and look Hugh in the face. "I love you and it hurt for so long when you didn't notice me. It ate me up inside and left a hole, but now, the way you are with me fills that space." He looked at Hugh imploringly. "Do you love me?"

"I'm not sure I understand what that means." Hugh breathed in deeply. "I understand a mother's desire to protect and provide for her young no matter the cost to herself. I understand a lion's loyalty to his pride. That's natural to us in all forms. But what you're describing..."

"Nobody talked to me growing up," Johnnie said. "They protected me because I'm a Siphon, but they weren't interested in me as a person, and even though it bothered me, it was mostly okay because I always sensed there would be something more. When I saw you, I knew you were that something. That's why it hurt so much when you didn't really see me. That's why—"

Hugh tugged Johnnie close and held on to him tightly. "I'm sorry," he mumbled, his lips pressed to the top of Johnnie's head. "I'm so sorry."

"I know," Johnnie assured him. "I'm not upset about it. I'm just explaining love." He tried to think of the right words.

"All I've ever wanted, all I want now, is you. I want to talk with you, look at you, smell you. I want you to smile and laugh and I want to be the reason for it. I want you to touch me and kiss me." He sighed in frustration, the words inadequate to explain the powerful emotion strumming through him. "That's love." He tipped his head back and looked at Hugh expectantly.

Seconds ticked by as Hugh gazed at Johnnie. "I said it was about keeping you warm but the truth is the best part of my day is falling asleep with you curled up against me and waking up the same way. Holding on to you makes me warm too." Hugh rubbed his palm over his chest. "In here."

Nodding, Johnnie blinked rapidly and then tucked his head under Hugh's chin and wiggled as close as he could to Hugh's broad body. His imagination hadn't run away with him. The emotion he had sensed coming from Hugh, the affection he had seen on Hugh's face, and the interest Hugh had shown in him were real.

"I want you to take your things out of your room and put them with mine so I know I'm going to be sleeping with you every night. I want this to be *our* bed. I want you with me every second of every day so I can see you and talk to you and smell you. Having you carry my power is just a side benefit." Hugh rubbed Johnnie's back gently. "Is that love?"

After clearing his throat, Johnnie rasped, "It's different for everyone but I'd like to think so."

"Me too," Hugh whispered.

"I have another question," Johnnie said, hoping Hugh

would indulge him further and not be frustrated by his probing.

"You can ask me anything, now and any other time." Hugh tangled his fingers in the back of Johnnie's hair and tugged his head back until their eyes met, then he caressed the back of Johnnie's head. "You're mine."

"Your Siphon." Johnnie nodded in agreement.

Hugh's chest rumbled. "What do you want to know?"

"You didn't tell Percy or the rest of the pride that we don't have to stay as close to each other anymore. You didn't explain that that was why Larry and Dennis didn't succeed in destroying you with your power."

"Shifters need to see their Premier as all-powerful and all-knowing to feel safe." Hugh lowered his hand to Johnnie's nape and massaged it. "The health and well-being of the pride depends on me being able to care for them."

"I'm sorry for what I did." Ashamed, Johnnie glanced away. "I know now how I endangered you and everyone else by making you appear vulnerable."

"It wasn't your fault. The responsibility for what you went through, what you felt you had to do, and what happened since all lie squarely on me. I should've seen that you were hurting." He sighed. "I should've seen a lot of things." He shook his head. "The point is, we're still figuring out what changed and why you can now carry my power even if we're not connected by sight or hearing or a small space. Telling the pride something so fundamental has changed won't give them comfort if I can't explain the reason for it. It'll make them question my knowledge, which will leave them feeling vulnerable."

The answer made perfect sense and it quieted the last of Johnnie's anxiety about how Hugh felt for him. "I think I have an idea about what changed."

"Already?" Hugh's dark eyes filled with admiration. "You're the most insightful shifter I've come across in over a century walking this earth."

"I'm not sure I'm right about it," Johnnie said, uncomfortable at the unfamiliar praise even though it warmed his heart. "It's just a theory."

"I'd like to hear your theory." Hugh's deep voice went soft.

"We've always known that for your power to flow into me and stay accessible to you, we had to be connected, and we assumed the connection had to be spatial or visual or auditory, right?" Johnnie flicked his gaze to Hugh, who nodded encouragingly, so he continued. "But what if it's not that limited?"

"What else is there?" Hugh asked. "If we're not close together and we can't see each other or hear each other, how can we be connected?"

"What if—" Johnnie ran his tongue over his lips and cleared his throat. "What if the connection can be emotional?"

Hugh continued looking at him, his expression intense and thoughtful.

"What if everything is related?" Johnnie continued. "You said sex with me feels different."

"It feels so good with you, Johnnie," Hugh rasped. "Nothing has ever made my body experience the kind of pleasure I do with you or the sense of fulfillment. I've spent myself with a dozen lions in a night and not felt sated, but one time with you and I'm drained, my seed and my tension." Hugh brushed his lips over Johnnie's and then nipped the lower one. "So, yes, that's different."

Trying to ignore the blood rushing to his cock, Johnnie said, "Maybe our emotional connection is tied together with our physical connection." He couldn't stop himself from rocking forward and rubbing his erection against Hugh's belly.

"Like the humans' making love idea." Hugh reached between them and circled his palm around Johnnie's dick.

"Yes," Johnnie squeaked. He took in several deep breaths and told himself to focus on what might be the most important conversation he'd ever had. "And maybe the connection between the two of us that transfers your power, maybe that connection can be emotional instead of physical. Maybe the closer we get in here"—Johnnie laid his palm over Hugh's heart—"the more connected we are regardless of how far apart our bodies get."

"That makes a lot of sense."

"Really?" Johnnie said, surprised despite having been the one who thought of the idea.

"Really." Hugh kissed Johnnie again, this time licking his way into Johnnie's mouth before drawing back and gently pressing their lips together over and over. "You're brilliant."

CHAPTER 15

"I LIKE being connected with you, Johnnie." Hugh slowly moved his hand up and down Johnnie's hard shaft.

"Ah!" Johnnie cried out when Hugh's thumb swiped over his glans. "Me too," he said breathlessly.

With his forehead, Hugh nudged Johnnie's head to the side, and then licked and sucked his way across Johnnie's neck. "There's another way I've been wanting to connect."

"Okay," Johnnie said breathlessly as he thrust his hips in counterpoint to Hugh's fist.

His voice taking on a tinge of amusement, Hugh said, "Don't you want to know what kind of connection?"

"What kind of connection," Johnnie repeated more than asked. The answer wouldn't matter because he'd do anything that got him closer to the big powerful man who had been the subject of his every fantasy and desire.

As Hugh moved his huge hand down Johnnie's shaft and over his balls, he said, "I want to connect in here." He slid his fingers through Johnnie's channel and then circled one fingertip over the wrinkled skin of his pucker. "I want to f—" Hugh paused and gazed at Johnnie for several long moments before speaking again, and when he did, his voice was low and gravelly. "I want to make love to you."

"Okay," Johnnie agreed.

Gently, Hugh tipped Johnnie onto his back and then leaned over him as he continued moving his fingers over Johnnie's sensitive skin. "I've been craving this." He kissed Johnnie. "With you."

"Why haven't you done it?" Johnnie spread his legs and tilted his hips up, making himself accessible. "You can do anything with me. I'm yours, remember?"

Moaning, Hugh ran his hands over Johnnie's body. "Because you're young and inexperienced and I'm not a small man."

As Hugh sat beside him, Johnnie dragged his gaze over Hugh's dark muscles and eventually settled his focus on Hugh's groin. His full balls hung low under a thick, veined shaft that was so heavy, gravity pulled it down. There was no disputing Hugh's size or his own lack of experience, and while twenty-six was well past the age when shifters left their mothers' dens and lived with other adults, compared to a person born in 1912, Johnnie would always be young.

"That's true." Johnnie reached his hand into Hugh's lap and gently fondled his dick. "But you said you want me despite those things, right?"

"Yes," Hugh hissed as he closed his eyes. "I want you so much that I don't know how I'll drain my seed with anyone else again."

Anger, hot and bright, surged through Johnnie.

Hugh's eyes snapped open. "What was that sound?"

With his jaw clenched tightly to the point of pain, Johnnie couldn't answer.

"You growled at me."

Instinctively, Johnnie shook his head. A lion didn't growl at his Premier.

"Yes, you did." Hugh grinned at him. "And you can relax your grip a little there." He flicked his gaze to his groin, where Johnnie held his balls. "My nuts aren't going anywhere."

"Sorry," Johnnie mumbled in embarrassment. He gentled his hold and carefully slid his fingers over Hugh's sac in apology.

"Tell me what's going on in your head."

Though he didn't want to confess an emotion that was distinctly not natural for shifters, his desire to be honest with Hugh, always and in all things, overrode his shame. "I was jealous of you having sex with anyone else."

"Jealous?" Hugh studied Johnnie's face. "Why?"

Of course Hugh wouldn't understand. Unlike humans, who joined in pairs and created family units, or wild lions, who lived in small groups where the few males mated with most of the females, lion shifters lived in prides as large as their leader could handle and had frequent sex with their pridemates, regardless of gender. A Premier Pride, especially one led by a Premier as experienced and powerful as Hugh, often had over a thousand adult lions and, other than females who were interested in getting pregnant, those adults fucked one another with the same casualness and ease as a simple conversation or a handshake.

"It's part of that making love concept we were talking about," Johnnie explained. "When humans love each other enough that they think of sex as making love, they usually don't do it with anyone else."

"I don't interact much with humans," Hugh said. "But I've been around enough of them to know they're not monogamous."

"Not all of them," Johnnie agreed. "But some of them are." He swallowed hard, drew in a deep breath, and gathered his courage. "I want to be." Johnnie looked into Hugh's eyes. "I don't want to have sex with anyone other than you."

A loud rumble sounded from Hugh's chest. He curled his lips, bared his teeth, narrowed his eyes, and raised his shoulders, like a lion readying himself for a fight.

"Hugh?" Johnnie asked worriedly.

Faster than Johnnie's eyes could track, Hugh pounced. He lay on top of Johnnie, pinning him to the bed. "You're mine," he growled, and then he clamped his teeth onto Johnnie's throat, not breaking skin, but holding him tight enough that Johnnie couldn't escape. Not that he wanted to do anything of the sort.

"Yes." Johnnie tipped his chin up and gave Hugh more room. "I'm your Siphon."

When Hugh removed his mouth, his jaw ticked and his nostrils flared. "Not just as a Siphon. All of you. I want all of you for myself."

"We're saying the same thing," Johnnie said breathlessly, his arousal shooting up sharply. "I understand your duty to lead and protect the pride and I understand my role in that now, but I want this"—Johnnie moved his hands over Hugh's nude chest and shoulders—"to be just between us." He gazed into Hugh's eyes and watched him carefully, needing to assure himself that his next question would be answered truthfully. "Can I be enough for you?"

"Yes," Hugh responded without hesitation. He paused, seemed to think it over, and then said, "Definitely." His brow crinkled. "Which is unusual. Not just because shifters aren't monogamous but also because fucking one lion has never been enough to drain my seed. But with you..." Hugh dragged his lips over Johnnie's forehead, down the bridge of his nose, and over his mouth. "Being with you calms me soul deep. We don't even have to fuck for me to be sated."

"But we're going to, right?" Johnnie asked. His pucker tingled in response to the way Hugh had been touching it and he wanted more. Based on the stiffness of Hugh's dick poking his thigh, he was certain the feeling was mutual. "You said you wanted to."

Instead of answering, Hugh buried his face in Johnnie's neck and inhaled. "I love the way you smell." He breathed in deeply. "Like citrus and lavender." He swiped his tongue across Johnnie's skin. "You taste good too." Slowly, he returned his hand to its spot between Johnnie's legs and slid his fingers into Johnnie's crease.

"Ah," Johnnie gasped.

"That's a happy sound, right?"

"Uh-huh." Johnnie nodded and folded his legs up on

either side of Hugh, planting his feet on the bed. "Feels so good when you touch me there."

"I'm glad." Hugh kissed him softly. "Because I like touching you here." He rubbed the hidden area. "Your skin is smooth and warm." He skated his fingertip over Johnnie's pucker, making him gasp. "And really sensitive."

Hugh lay over Johnnie, tucked between his spread knees, braced on one forearm, touching him intimately. He watched Johnnie intently, and Johnnie returned his gaze, enjoying the tenderness in the usually impassive face.

"Before, I fucked to drain away tension and hormones," Hugh said. "I did it to keep myself sane and calm. But making love must be different because I want to taste you." He lowered his face to Johnnie's chest and lapped at his nipple before taking it between his lips and sucking. "I want to explore every inch of you." Hugh moved to Johnnie's other nipple, swirled his tongue around it, and then took it into his mouth. "I want to make you feel good."

"Hugh," Johnnie moaned, arching his chest.

"You taste delicious." Hugh kissed and licked his way down Johnnie's belly, over his hip, to his balls.

"Oh. Oh. Oh." Johnnie panted and writhed when Hugh flattened his tongue and smoothed it over his sac.

"Turn over," Hugh said, his voice gritty. He dropped his mouth over Johnnie's testicles and sucked them in.

"Ah!" Johnnie clawed at the mattress and thrust his hips up.

"Never mind." Hugh grasped Johnnie's thighs and

rolled him up until his knees were near his armpits and his spread ass faced the ceiling. "This position works too."

"What—"

Hugh nipped at Johnnie's butt, stealing his voice. He started at the fleshy part of Johnnie's ass and nibbled his way toward the center, occasionally flicking his tongue or sucking up a mark. When he reached Johnnie's channel, he flattened his tongue and licked from the base of Johnnie's spine to his perineum.

"Ungh," Johnnie moaned as Hugh explored every inch of his crease with lips and tongue. "Hugh."

"I can't get enough of you," Hugh said quietly. He traced Johnnie's hole with the tip of his tongue. "Tasting you here makes my dick so hard, Johnnie." He pressed the tip against the center of Johnnie's hole, pushed it inside, and flicked it. "So wonderfully hard." In and out he went, deeper every time, until eventually he pushed his lips against Johnnie's hole and plunged his tongue as far as it could go.

With every movement of the slick muscle within his body, Johnnie climbed closer and closer toward orgasm. His moans became louder and more desperate. He grabbed the backs of his thighs and spread his legs even farther. Though he wanted to encourage Hugh, Johnnie was too turned on to speak. All he could do was stare at Hugh as he worked him with mouth, tongue, and hands.

"I want to make you come like this someday, but right now, I think I'll lose my mind if I don't get inside you." Hugh cupped each side of Johnnie's ass, massaged the firm globes, and then slid both of his thumbs inside. "I've never wanted anything this much."

With two digits buried in Johnnie's ass, Hugh rose and gently kissed him. "I want to give you pleasure," he said as he pumped in and out of Johnnie's hole.

"You are," Johnnie assured him, arousal making his words thick and slow.

After another few seconds gazing into Johnnie's face and fingering his ass, Hugh leaned toward the nightstand and retrieved a bottle of lubricant. Kneeling between Johnnie's thighs, he propped Johnnie's ankles on his shoulders, drizzled the slick liquid onto his channel, and pushed it inside. Once Johnnie was slippery, Hugh rubbed the lube onto his own shaft.

"Part of me wishes more than anything that you'd had a normal life and been included in the pride like the rest of the lions." Hugh pressed the tip of his cock against Johnnie's hole. "But the selfish part of me is glad you didn't because it means I'm the first person who gets to do this with you." He gripped Johnnie's hips, gazed into his eyes, and slowly pressed inside. "The *only* person."

"Never wanted a normal life," Johnnie bit out, his words strained. He curled his hands around Hugh's forearms and held on. "Just wanted you."

"You have me, Johnnie." Hugh continued his even, deliberate slide until his balls squished against Johnnie's ass. "You have all of me."

"Oh Lord." Johnnie's eyes rolled back and his mouth

dropped open. The stimulation of previously untouched nerve endings stole his breath. "That's so good."

"For me too." Hugh moved Johnnie's legs off his shoulders to around his waist and then planted his hands on either side of Johnnie's torso and began rocking his hips. "You feel... Ungh," Hugh groaned.

"Kiss me," Johnnie whispered, suddenly needing more contact. He curled his palms around Hugh's neck and tugged. "Please kiss me."

Without any hesitation, Hugh lowered his face, pressed his lips to Johnnie's, and slipped his tongue inside. As soon as their flavors blended, both men moaned. Though the pace of Hugh's thrusts stayed the same, the sensation in Johnnie's passage became more pronounced. He felt as though dozens of tiny fingers were caressing him and every time Hugh dragged his cock past Johnnie's prostate, those fingers tapped it one by one.

"Johnnie," Hugh said, his voice hoarse, breathless, and confused. "Something's different." In and out he went, not slowing down or speeding up. "My cock is..." He arched his neck and gasped. "There's more... I feel it everywhere... I..." Leaving one hand to hold himself up, he slipped his other between their bodies until he reached the area where they were connected. "What is that?"

"Please don't stop." Johnnie had no idea how to answer Hugh's question. He had nothing to compare to this moment so he couldn't know if it was different, but he had never felt anything so powerful, so exquisite, so fundamentally right, and he didn't want it to end. "Please, Hugh, don't stop."

"I won't," Hugh promised. "I can't. But—" Without ceasing his back and forth movement inside Johnnie, Hugh rose to his knees and glanced at their joined bodies. "Holy hell." He jerked his gaze up to Johnnie's face and then back down. "How?"

Awash in sensation and pleasure, Johnnie had trouble concentrating and speaking, but he managed a weak, "What?"

"I have spines." Hugh slowed his movements to a crawl, as if to let Johnnie feel every inch of his dick pushing in. "That only happens in lion form. Besides, I'm a Premier. Our cocks never grow spines because they're for procreation." He slid out just as slowly. "I don't understand."

"I don't either," Johnnie said. And his mind was too clouded with lust and need to figure it out. "We can think about it later." He pushed his ass toward Hugh, hoping for more contact. "But right now, it feels incredible." When Hugh snapped in again, his angle shifted so the spines dragged over new parts of Johnnie's internal walls and then over his gland. He trembled from head to toe and cried out Hugh's name.

"Look at you," Hugh rasped. "So beautiful." He lowered himself over Johnnie, curled his hands under Johnnie's arms, grasped his shoulders, and began pumping in earnest. "You're gorgeous, Johnnie, inside and out." Sweat shone over Hugh's dark brow. "And you make me feel so good. This is so so good."

As Hugh moved above him and inside him, Johnnie

stared at his handsome, strong face, inhaled his spicy scent, and gave his body over to pleasure so profound he was sure he'd been made for this very purpose, for this very man.

"Yours," he whispered.

"Yes." Hugh pulled all the way out and then slammed back in. "Mine." He wrenched his dick out and then shoved inside again. "My Siphon." Out and back in. "My Johnnie." His nostrils flaring, gaze glued to Johnnie's face, and lips parted, he slowly pulled out until only his crown was inside. "My love."

"Hugh," Johnnie choked, his throat thick with emotion. "I love you."

With a nod, Hugh lowered his face and slanted his mouth over Johnnie's. He moaned and sucked on Johnnie's tongue voraciously while he snapped his hips harder and faster, over and over, until Johnnie screamed into his mouth from the force of his orgasm. Seed sprayed between them, coating their skin in Johnnie's essence as white-hot pleasure tore through his body and brain.

"Yes!" Hugh yelled triumphantly. "Lord, yes." He buried his cock to the base and ground against Johnnie, his balls rubbing against Johnnie's backside as they emptied deep inside him. "Yes," he said quietly, his eyes closed and face slack. "Yes."

After several long moments gasping for air and clinging to Johnnie, Hugh kissed his cheek, his jaw, his neck, and his chest. He then rolled onto his side, pulled Johnnie into his arms, and brushed his lips over the top of Johnnie's head.

"What was that?" he asked breathlessly. "I've never experienced anything like it." He squeezed Johnnie tightly. "Never."

"It sounded different." Though Johnnie had never personally experienced penetration, he had watched Hugh screw hundreds of times, always longing to be the lion underneath him.

"Completely different." Hugh breathed in deeply, sounding satisfied. "What we just did bears only a surface resemblance to sex as I know it."

Based on Hugh's noises and expressions while they were coming together, Johnnie knew that was true. The man he'd seen rutting with others had been stoic and robotic, focused on his end goal but not deriving pleasure from his task. But when the two of them were joined together, Hugh's face had been awash in yearning and joy.

"I understand what you mean now about making love." Hugh nudged Johnnie's head until he looked up and their gazes met. "Do you think that's why I had spines?"

"That's never happened before, right?" Johnnie asked as he thought over the question.

"No." He shook his head. "Even though I haven't come across many Premiers, over the years, I have met some. A few, I'd even consider friends. And of course I've heard stories about our ancestors. As far as I know, male shifters develop spines on their cocks during sex in lion form to help the female get pregnant. I've never seen it happen in human form, I've never heard them say it feels special, and I've never heard of it happening to a Premier."

"Because you can't procreate?"

"That's what I thought."

"Well"—Johnnie moved his hand to Hugh's groin and gently fondled him—"this isn't the first time your body reacted..." He tried to think of the right word. "Differently to sex with me."

"It isn't only sex. You're special, Johnnie." Hugh traced his thumb over Johnnie's jawline. "Talking is different with you. Sharing meals is different with you. Sleeping is different with you." Hugh paused and gazed into his eyes. "*I'm* different with you."

"I'm different with you too," Johnnie answered, his voice cracking. "I'm whole now. I'm happy."

Hugh wrapped his arms around him and pulled him into a tight hug.

"Maybe it's as simple as that."

"What?" Hugh asked.

"Maybe—" Johnnie licked his lips and thought over what he was about to say. Wanting something as much as he wanted Hugh, made objectivity impossible. "I mean, I could be wrong. It could be wishful thinking, but—" He sucked in air and then let the words spill out. "Maybe we were meant to be together. Maybe our bodies were made for each other. Maybe this is what we were supposed to be and do all along and that's why it feels good and right and whole and..." He ran out of air, sighed, and whispered, "Maybe."

"Maybe," Hugh repeated, his lips turned up at the

corners and his eyes looking happy.

"You're not upset about that?"

"Why would I be upset that an incredibly intelligent, handsome, sweet person was made for me?" Hugh shook his head. "That might not have been my... What did you call it? A wish? But that's only because I've never thought about wishing for something for myself. Everything I've done or wanted has been for the pride. That's what a Premier is for— the pride."

The only Premier Johnnie knew was Hugh and there was no doubt about his devotion to his lions. He worked to ensure their safety and happiness all day, every day. And Johnnie spent that time focused on Hugh, devoted to Hugh.

"That could be true. A Premier could be for the pride," Johnnie said. "And a Siphon could be for the Premier."

"Could be." Hugh smiled at Johnnie, brushed his hair off his forehead, and leaned in for a kiss. "My brilliant Siphon." Their lips met time and again, softly, tenderly. "My precious gift."

For so many years the word *Siphon* had evoked feelings of resentment, loneliness, and frustration in Johnnie, but now, being cradled in his Premier's muscular arms and held close to his huge body, Johnnie felt fortunate to have been born for this role, for this pride, for this Premier. Joy, affection, purpose, and pleasure filled his life now. He wouldn't give that up and he wouldn't let anyone take it from him. He wouldn't let anyone take Hugh.

CHAPTER 16

"I'M not a weakling," Johnnie said as he stood from the table and took their dishes to the sink. He began washing them and kept his back to Hugh, hiding his face so Hugh couldn't see his humiliation. He wasn't a seven foot, three hundred pound Premier lion, but at almost six feet tall and one hundred sixty pounds, Johnnie was strong and capable. He wished Hugh saw him that way.

"Of course you're not weak, Johnnie. And if it was you against either one of them, you'd be evenly matched. But it's two against one."

"Or more than two," Johnnie muttered.

"What?"

Johnnie sighed, put the last plate on the dishrack, and dried his hands. "Last time they tried to take me with two men and it didn't work. If they have any sense, they'll come back with reinforcements."

"You make a good point, as usual. And it supports my position that this is a bad idea." Hugh pushed his chair back, the legs scraping against the wood floor, and then footsteps sounded behind Johnnie. "I'm not letting you put yourself out as bait for Larry and Dennis." Large arms circled around

Johnnie's chest and then Hugh's breath blew across his neck. "I don't want you to be hurt."

"Are you ready for my next point?" Johnnie laid his arms over Hugh's and threaded their fingers together. Though he was a bit resentful that Hugh didn't think he could take care of himself, the genuine concern in Hugh's voice and the feeling of Hugh's hard body pressed against his, made it impossible for him to be truly angry.

"Yes," Hugh said grudgingly.

"Larry and Dennis don't know my purring heals us or about our ability to be separated for a longer distance. That gives us an advantage, a *huge* advantage. They can't hurt me."

"They absolutely *can* hurt you," Hugh snapped. He grasped Johnnie's shoulders and spun him around. "They in fact *did* hurt you. And they could kill you. Maybe not as easily as they could kill another lion, but if that's their goal and they have access to you, they *can* do it."

Now that he understood the importance of the pride's perception of their Premier as ever-confident, Johnnie was glad nobody else was there to witness Hugh's terrified expression. "Their goal isn't to kill me," Johnnie reminded him softly. "Their goal is to kill you by separating us." He turned his head to the side and kissed Hugh's forearm. "But we know that won't work. Our connection isn't based only on proximity now. It's physical."

"This is more than physical," Hugh said, his voice gruff. He moved his hands to Johnnie's neck and rubbed it with his thick, long fingers.

"You're right." Johnnie caressed Hugh's chest and felt warmth bloom in his. "It's also emotional and mental. We have a lot of connections, Hugh. They can't break us."

"No, they can't," Hugh agreed. "But you're not invincible and I won't risk you. I know you're upset but..." He placed his fingers under Johnnie's chin, tipped his head back, and searched his eyes. "I don't want you to hurt. Can you understand that?"

"I can." Johnnie nodded. "But it's our best option."

"They may have given up," Hugh said, not sounding convinced by his own suggestion.

"Even if they want to give up, which I doubt, they can't. At this point, they have to hide from everyone in Berk and any other pride because otherwise you'll find them. If they try to live on their own, they won't survive because shifters need to be part of a pride. You said it yourself, they're dead men walking. With death as their only alternative, of course they'll try to kill you and take over Berk."

"Then we can wait them out. That's an option," Hugh said tiredly.

"We've been waiting for two weeks." Johnnie brushed his palm over Hugh's chest. "The entire pride is on edge, unsure what's going to happen, and nervous as they wait for it. They feed on each other's anxiety and the stress level is getting higher every day."

"I know." Hugh turned on his heel and walked to the other side of the kitchen, rubbing his hand over his head.

Of course Hugh knew. As devoted as he was to the pride,

he wouldn't miss their mounting panic, and as their Premier, he couldn't let that kind of unrest continue. Confident Hugh would ultimately agree they had to draw Larry and Dennis out rather than continuing to wait for them to make a move, Johnnie leaned against the counter and quietly watched Hugh pace.

After a few minutes, Hugh slumped his shoulders resignedly, dropped onto a chair, and said, "Tell me your plan."

"There isn't a lot of detail to it," Johnnie admitted. "Basically, I should be accessible to them and they need to know that." He walked over to Hugh, who spread his knees wide, making room for Johnnie between them. "If I'm right that Larry is biding his time, waiting for an opportunity to get to me when you're not around, then we should give him the opportunity and do it in a way that'll let him know it's coming."

"How can he know?" Hugh's posture stiffened, his dark eyes narrowed, and his nostrils flared. "You think someone in my pride is feeding him information?"

"Absolutely not." Johnnie vehemently shook his head. "I think he's staying close enough that he'll catch wind of well-placed information, but there's no way anyone in Berk would intentionally tell him anything. Every member of this pride is loyal to you."

"Except Dennis."

Though Hugh would never admit it and he tried to hide it, Johnnie knew Hugh well enough to hear the hurt in that statement.

"Dennis is loyal to you." Johnnie climbed onto Hugh's big lap, draped his legs on either side of his torso, and wound his arms around Hugh's neck. In that position, they were eye-to-eye and Johnnie relished the tenderness in Hugh's expression as he gazed at him. "He made a mistake." Guilt washed over Johnnie as he remembered the cause of that mistake. "It's my fault. I made him think the pride was at risk so he—"

"He should have come to me if he had concerns." Hugh cupped Johnnie's cheeks and caressed them with this thumbs. "You're not responsible for Dennis's poor decisions."

"He wouldn't have done any of this if I hadn't tried to hang myself and made him doubt you."

"You wouldn't have tried to"—Hugh ground his teeth, swallowed hard, and rasped—"do what you did if I had been paying attention to you, taking care of you." He brushed his lips over Johnnie's cheek, the gesture feeling like both affection and an apology. "I didn't do right by you and you suffered the consequences." Hugh took a deep breath. "Dennis Jones is thirty-five years old. He was born in Berk. I've been his Premier his entire life. I was his mother's Premier all of her life and even his grandmother's Premier for most of hers. In all those years, Berk has never been in danger and our members have never needed for anything. This is a good pride, a strong pride. I gave Dennis a good life." Hugh's voice got deeper, angrier. "He should have trusted in me, but instead he betrayed me and our pride. The fault for that lies squarely on his shoulders. Nobody else's."

Though Johnnie wouldn't forget the role he had played in creating their current predicament, neither could he dispute the truth of Hugh's statements. But dwelling on the past wasn't productive and wouldn't bring them closer to a peaceful future. A solid plan was what they needed, so that was where he'd put his focus.

"The festival grounds are a perfect location," Johnnie mumbled, an idea coalescing in his mind.

"A perfect location for what?"

After taking a few more seconds to let the concept crystalize, Johnnie said, "A perfect location for a pride gathering, one we start talking about now." He paused. "Thanksgiving is less than two weeks away. That weekend's a perfect time to do this."

Smiling fondly, Hugh said, "I'll just sit here while you get this worked out and then you can fill me in on my role."

"Oh." Johnnie's neck heated. "Sorry. I was focused on the thinking part and skipped the explaining part."

"I could see that." Hugh slid his fingers over Johnnie's nape and up into his hair. "Your mind is sharp and watching it work is..." He crinkled his brow and seemed to search for the right words. "The way you think is sexy."

Johnnie's groin tightened and his breathing quickened. "My thinking is sexy?"

Nodding, Hugh said, "Among other things. There's a lot about you that's sexy." He tugged on Johnnie's hair until he raised his chin, exposing his throat, and then he leaned forward and licked a swath up Johnnie's neck. "Your intelligence is high on the list but so is your tight, talented body."

"Talented?" Johnnie asked hoarsely.

"I never even imagined the possibility of the pleasure your body gives me, Johnnie. Everything about you turns me on." Hugh skimmed his hands down Johnnie's back, clutched his ass, and pulled him forward against his hot erection.

Forcing himself to be responsible despite yearning for what Hugh offered, Johnnie said, "We should talk about the plan." Or he could unfasten both of their pants, free their cocks, and rub up against Hugh. Or he could slide off Hugh's lap, kneel between his knees, and take his thick rod deep into his mouth. Or he could undress from the waist down, bend over the table and—

"If you want me to understand anything important, you need to stop moaning and rocking against me." Hugh nipped at Johnnie's earlobe. "Those needy sounds and movements make me so damn hard my brain must be short on blood."

"Sorry." Johnnie dropped his forehead onto Hugh's shoulder and took long, slow breaths. "Your touch completely distracts me from"—he trembled and wiggled closer to Hugh—"everything else."

"Mmm," Hugh hummed happily. "I like that I can make you feel good enough to penetrate that iron focus." He massaged Johnnie's ass, digging his fingers into the muscular globes. "But this conversation is important so how about we compromise?"

"Compromise?" Johnnie raised his head and blinked at Hugh, trying to follow along through the thick haze of lust that surrounded him whenever those big hands touched him.

"Yes. We slow this down, talk about your plan, and when that's all worked out, we make love."

Johnnie warmed at how fully his century-old Premier, whose life had been focused exclusively on caring for a lion shifter pride, had embraced a concept normally foreign to their kind. Overwhelmed by emotion, he buried his face in Hugh's neck, clung to him, and whispered, "I love you."

"I love you too." Hugh kissed the top of his head and held him while he regrouped.

After giving himself a few moments to enjoy the closeness, Johnnie sat up straight and cleared his throat. "So, the plan."

"Let's hear it." Hugh smiled. "You know I love your ideas."

Hugh always listened to Johnnie's thoughts and sought his opinion. Receiving respect and encouragement from the person he most admired bolstered Johnnie's confidence in himself. His idea had risks, but he was certain it'd work, so he took a deep breath and plunged ahead.

"The festival grounds abut undeveloped pride land, which leads to acres of National Forest Service land."

"Right."

"And unless we're having a large gathering, that part of the pride lands is generally vacant."

"You think Dennis and his friend are camping out in

the festival grounds?"

"No." Johnnie shook his head. "That's too close to us, and I don't think they'd risk being caught, but you know how you said when you hunt you go where the prey is going to be instead of where they are?"

Hugh nodded.

"Well, I did what you said. I considered all the factors and I suspect they're on Forest Service land abutting the pride lands. Close but not too close. And I think I know where they'll be." Johnnie cleared his throat. "Or at least where they'll be if we set them up to be there."

"You want to set them up to be at the festival grounds by having an all pride event?"

"Yes. If they're keeping an eye on things from a distance and we start gearing up for something that big, they're bound to catch wind of it." And Johnnie was certain that was exactly what Larry and Dennis were doing. "During the last pride festival, Larry saw me apart from you. We can do that again. By Thanksgiving, they'll have been on their own, without a pride or resources for a month. My bet is they'll be desperate enough to take a chance and try to get to me."

"If either of them step into the middle of a pride event, they'll be killed. They have to know that or they'd have already approached a pride member."

"I agree, which is why I'll be on the periphery. If we leave some empty space in the portion of the festival grounds closest to the Forest Service land, they can walk from that land, onto the undeveloped pride land and get to me without making contact with anyone else."

Slowly, Hugh nodded. "And then I'll kill them."

Johnnie winced.

His expression softening, Hugh said, "There's no other choice, Johnnie. As long as they're alive, they pose a danger to Berk, and even if they give up on our pride and decide to try a takeover somewhere else, another pride will be at risk."

Johnnie knew Hugh couldn't allow his lions to be hurt and that he was an old enough and strong enough Premier to feel a sense of responsibility for other prides as well.

"And also—" Hugh sighed. "Lion shifters prosper and flourish when they feel safe. A strong Premier is key to that and I cannot send a message that I will tolerate acts of violence against our pride."

That type of message was exactly what had gotten them into their current predicament, only Hugh hadn't been the one to send it. The blame for that lay with Johnnie, even if Hugh didn't hold it against him.

"I understand," Johnnie said. "It's not Larry I'm worried about."

"You're looking out for Dennis because he was a member of Berk." Hugh cupped Johnnie's jaw and kissed him tenderly. "Despite everything you went through and everything he did to you, you remain loyal."

In truth, Johnnie's loyalty lay solely with Hugh. He understood the magnitude of Hugh's drive to protect his pride and he was certain that killing a member of Berk, even a former member, would pain Hugh. *That* was what worried him.

"I wish it didn't have to be like this," Johnnie said.

"I do too and in a Premier Pride, especially one the size of ours, lions are content with their lives, so disputes don't escalate and minor disagreements are quickly forgotten. But most prides are smaller with limited resources. Their lions are constantly on edge and defensive. They regularly battle one another and other prides." Hugh looked away. "You were too young and secluded to have seen much of that before Westgate merged into Berk, but it's the way of nature. When our home, our safety, or our pride is threatened, we eliminate the challenger to ensure our security. I've been around long enough to see it time and time again, which is why I constantly work to shelter our pride from upheaval." He slowly moved his thumb up and down Johnnie's neck, the barely-there touch calming. "Right now, that means getting rid of Larry and Dennis so our lions are reassured of their safety and interlopers get the message that Berk is an impenetrable target they should avoid. I'm the Premier; it's my duty to do that."

"Okay." Johnnie turned his head to the side and kissed Hugh's palm. Everything Hugh said was true, but he still had a couple of weeks to analyze their plan and maybe he'd be able to come up with a way for Hugh to protect his pride without hurting his soul.

CHAPTER 17

"You're up early," Johnnie said as he undulated his hips and rubbed his ass against Hugh's erection.

"I was up while I was sleeping." Hugh snaked his hand around Johnnie's waist and flattened his palm on Johnnie's belly. "You do that to me." He pressed his face to Johnnie's neck and inhaled. "Your scent makes me hard." He gently rocked, dragging his thick cock through Johnnie's crease. "Being naked, curled around you, skin to skin turns me on." He parted his lips and sucked on Johnnie's nape. "Feels so good to want like this."

Desire flooded Johnnie, sharp and sweet. Bending one knee toward his chest, he opened himself to Hugh. "I want you too," he said, squeezing and releasing his hole reflexively in anticipation of the delicious stretch Hugh would soon give him, the deep connection. "Inside."

"We'll get there." Hugh kissed his way across Johnnie's shoulders. "Need to taste you first." He rolled Johnnie onto his belly, straddled his thighs, and caressed his back, fingers digging into the muscles. "You have the best skin. Soft and warm."

"You make me warm from the inside." For years,

Johnnie had felt icy no matter the temperature or what he wore, but now Hugh filled the emptiness within him and chased away the chill.

Hot breath ghosted over Johnnie's shoulder blade before Hugh's slick tongue lapped at him. "Mmm," Hugh moaned. "Delicious." He traced the bone from top to bottom, then flattened his tongue and licked his way down Johnnie's spine. "My beautiful Siphon." As he kissed Johnnie's rounded globes and the sensitive area where ass met thigh, he pried Johnnie's legs apart and settled between them. "I love you." The words were barely a whisper, as if Hugh's feelings seeped out. He cupped either side of Johnnie's ass, spread him open, and then dipped forward and licked the hidden skin.

"Ah!" Johnnie gasped. Keeping his shoulders on the bed, he raised his ass and gave Hugh more room to pleasure him.

"Good?" Hugh asked and then twirled the tip of his tongue over the perimeter of Johnnie's rosebud.

"Uh-huh," Johnnie answered breathlessly. "I like that." He more than liked it, but words escaped him.

"I do too." Hugh gently nipped on the puckered skin and then flicked his tongue over it. "I love how you push closer to my mouth and whimper, like you want more." Moving away from the needy spot, he ran his tongue from Johnnie's balls to the small of his back. "Do you want more?"

"Want you," Johnnie answered honestly. "Anything with you."

Hugh dropped his forehead to Johnnie's back and

caressed his flanks. "Lord," he sighed. "I want to be worthy of what you see in me."

After a few quiet moments, Hugh parted Johnnie's cheeks again. Only this time, when he pressed his mouth to Johnnie's hole, he slid his tongue inside, tantalizing Johnnie's nerve endings.

"Ungh," Johnnie moaned. "Yes."

Keeping his grip on Johnnie firm but not hard enough to hurt, Hugh continued loving him with his mouth, plunging his tongue in and out of his passage while opening and closing his lips over the sensitive skin outside it.

With every pass of Hugh's skilled tongue, Johnnie's arousal heightened and soon he was rocking back and forth against Hugh's face, gasping for air, and clutching the sheets. "Hugh," he cried out as his groin tightened almost painfully. "I need to come."

"I'll take you there." Hugh slid two fingers into Johnnie's saliva-slick passage, curled them, and pegged his gland.

"Oh." Johnnie's chest heaved, his balls hardened, and his cock dripped. "Oh. Oh. Oh."

Continuing his erotic assault on Johnnie's hole, Hugh curled his arm around Johnnie's hip and took hold of his dick. That final touch was all Johnnie needed to fall over the edge into a body-numbing orgasm. He shouted with each pulse of his cock and then closed his eyes and gulped in air as aftershocks racked his body.

"Look at you," Hugh whispered into Johnnie's ear as he curled his larger body over Johnnie's. "So beautiful when you come for me."

When his heart stopped trying to pound out of his chest, Johnnie opened his eyes and met a dark, heated gaze. Hugh's fingers were still buried inside him, but he now lay on his side with his leg flung over Hugh's hip.

"I thought you were going to"—Johnnie reached between them and wrapped his palm around Hugh's hot, hard shaft—"give me this."

"I will," Hugh said hoarsely. "But first I wanted to touch and taste you." He brushed his lips over Johnnie's. "You amaze me." He slowly moved his fingers in and out of Johnnie's hole. "You're resilient and intelligent and giving." With a pained whimper, he slanted his mouth over Johnnie's, slid his tongue inside, and kissed him hungrily. "I don't want you to get hurt today."

The all-pride Thanksgiving meal was that evening. When Hugh had announced the community celebration, everyone had been thrilled. It had been the talk of Berk for two weeks and during the last couple of days, pride members had worked to get the festival grounds ready, bringing noise and a flurry of activity to the area. If Larry and Dennis were watching Berk, they had to have heard about the event, which meant everything was going according to plan. But as the day approached, Hugh had kept Johnnie closer than usual, almost clinging to him, and while he enjoyed the affection, Johnnie didn't want Hugh to worry.

"I heal quickly," he assured Hugh once again.

"I know." Hugh kissed Johnnie again, this time sucking

on his tongue. "But I never want you to have pain." He skimmed his free hand over Johnnie's shoulders and back. "Not even a little." He sunk his fingers deep into Johnnie and rubbed his thumb back and forth over the soft skin between Johnnie's balls and hole. "I should be protecting you and instead I'm putting you in harm's way."

"I like that," Johnnie whispered.

"This?" Hugh curled his fingers against Johnnie's prostate at the same time he pushed his thumb down, putting pressure on the gland from the outside.

"Ungh," Johnnie moaned as his dick began hardening again. "I love the way you touch me, but I meant I like what you said."

"You like being put in harm's way?"

"I like that you want to protect me, that I'm important enough to you for my safety and feelings to matter. And you're not putting me in harm's way. You're letting me help end a problem I had a part in starting."

"I already told you none of this is your fault."

"Thank you." Hugh's belief didn't change the facts, but it did make Johnnie feel better, for which he was grateful. "Hugh?" he said, sliding his hand up Hugh's shaft.

"Yes."

"You'll be near me tonight, watching, protecting. I'll be fine."

Hugh grunted in acknowledgement, if not agreement.

"Can we stop talking now?" Nothing they said would change what they had to do that evening but they didn't need to leave the cocoon of their bed yet. "I need you." Johnnie squeezed his ass around Hugh's invading digits.

"I need you too." Hugh looked into Johnnie's eyes, his expression grave. "Don't forget that." He gulped and then said, "Please be careful tonight."

"I promise."

After another few seconds gazing at Johnnie, Hugh started scooting down the mattress.

"Where are you going?"

When his mouth was level with Johnnie's cock, Hugh said, "Here," and then twirled his tongue around Johnnie's glans.

"I want—"

"I know." Hugh wiggled his fingers inside Johnnie's hole. "I'll suck you first, get you hard, and then we'll make love."

Pride members occasionally looked at Johnnie strangely, and he suspected they were wondering the same thing Percy had mentioned in Hugh's office almost a month earlier—why was Hugh limiting himself to sex with one lion and how could that be enough? But nobody else had seen this side of Hugh—the attentive lover who preferred to care for his partner rather than rushing toward his own release. And nobody else would see it. Just like nobody else would see Hugh worrying about harm coming to the pride. To them, Hugh projected a caring, albeit stoic persona, the ever-confident, strong Premier. Only Johnnie saw the vulnerability and passion inside the man.

"Hugh?"

With his lips wrapped around Johnnie's cock, Hugh raised his gaze.

"I love you."

Hugh's eyes warmed, and he squeezed Johnnie's hip with his free hand as he dropped his mouth lower, taking Johnnie's length deep.

Pleasure and desire swirled inside Johnnie, making him hunger for more sensation, more connections, more of Hugh.

"I want to suck you too," he said as he reached for Hugh's head and shoulders, touching wherever he could reach. "Please."

Hugh swung his huge body around and curled his back so his dick was level with Johnnie's face.

With a lusty moan, Johnnie leaned forward and inhaled, absorbing Hugh's strong, masculine scent. He cupped one hand under Hugh's sac, the heavy balls barely fitting on his palm, and held his erection with the other. Thick and long with pulsing veins, Hugh's beautiful cock was worthy of being worshipped so that was what Johnnie set out to do. He took the crown into his mouth and sucked, drizzling his saliva down the shaft as he stroked it.

Reacting to Johnnie's actions, Hugh groaned around Johnnie's dick and pumped his fingers faster, adding friction to Johnnie's passage. As Hugh ramped up his ministrations, Johnnie's need elevated. They fed off one another, desire, passion, and pleasure growing until, with a growl, Hugh turned around, rolled on top of Johnnie, and slammed his mouth on Johnnie's. He drew voraciously on Johnnie's tongue, his hands everywhere, and then Johnnie heard fumbling on the nightstand moments before Hugh's lube-slick fingers plunged back into his hole.

"Hugh!" he shouted and tilted his hips up. "Yes!" He wrapped his legs around Hugh, propped his heels on Hugh's back, and rode his fingers.

Grunting and panting, Hugh fingered him quickly, slicked his own cock, and then sucked on Johnnie's neck as he punched his cock deep inside Johnnie's body.

Johnnie arched his back and neck and gasped for air, the penetration breath-stealingly perfect.

"So good," Hugh rasped. "Everything with you... everything about you...so good."

Within moments, Johnnie felt the erotic spines sprout from Hugh's dick, adding to the sensations of their coupling.

"Oh Lord." Hugh's eyes widened and his expression looked almost pained. "I'll never get used to that. So incredible." He moved faster, thrust harder, and drove into Johnnie with unyielding pressure and focus. "Tell me this isn't too much." He gasped for air. "Tell me you're enjoying it."

Even in this moment, with his hormones at a peak, Hugh thought of Johnnie and his needs.

"Yes." Johnnie blinked tears out of his eyes, the emotions between them overwhelming. "Give me more."

Roaring, Hugh rammed in and out, plundering Johnnie's hole and opening him up to endless pleasure. He slammed his mouth back on Johnnie's, biting, licking, and sucking on his lips. And just as Johnnie thought he couldn't fly any higher, Hugh took his nipple between his fingers and twisted it.

"Hugh!" Johnnie cried out as his body shook and seed shot from his dick in round after round of bliss.

He heard Hugh yell, felt him shove inside one final time, and then the big body above him trembled as Hugh held him close and came inside him.

"Johnnie," Hugh whispered. He combed his fingers through the hair at Johnnie's temples and gazed at him adoringly. "We're going to be careful at the festival so you stay whole and healthy and we can come home tonight and do this again."

Johnnie choked out a laugh, his lungs still heaving too hard for the sound to be loud. "That's great inspiration."

"Good." Hugh grinned and rubbed the tip of his nose against Johnnie's. "I'll use whatever incentive I can to make sure my Siphon stays safe."

CHAPTER 18

"Siphon!"

Johnnie stopped walking toward the perimeter of the festival grounds and turned around.

"I'm glad I caught you," said Alexandra Harris as she hurried over to him. "I noticed you didn't eat any green bean casserole so I made you a bowl." Once she neared, she thrust her hands forward, food in one and a bottle of water in the other.

Blinking in surprise, Johnnie looked down at the bowl she held and then back to her face.

"Van Hartwick said you enjoyed green beans when you and Hugh ate at his pride house and Amy Young told me the same thing so I made my famous green bean casserole for you." Her cheeks reddened and she glanced away. "I don't mean *famous* famous but everyone says they like it so…" She cleared her throat. "Anyway, I thought maybe with the buffet tables being so full you hadn't seen it and that's why you didn't eat any."

He had been distracted during the meal, blindly filling his plate and then barely picking at his food while he waited for a reasonable time to leave the main gathering area.

When some lions began clearing the tables to make room for dessert and several others stood to stretch their legs and drain their bladders, he made eye contact with Hugh, silently suggesting it was time to implement their plan. Once he got a tiny nod from his Premier, he got up and walked away, knowing Hugh would wait for a short time and then follow him at a distance. Certain his absence wouldn't be noticed by the pride in celebration mode, he had focused only on his targets and hadn't notice he was being followed.

"You made this for me?" he asked, flicking his gaze to the food.

"It's potluck so technically it's for everyone but I wanted to be sure I made something you'd like so I asked around." She pushed the bowl and bottle against Johnnie's chest and he instinctively took them.

"Why?" As soon as he asked the question, he recognized how rude it sounded. "I mean, uh, thank you. That's very thoughtful."

"I realize we don't know each other because you were always hidden before so we didn't see you, but now you're part of things so hopefully that'll change and we can be friends."

Alexandra had been a member of Berk before the merger, so her comment wasn't in reference to how Johnnie had been confined while his birth pride had waited for him to come of age. And though Johnnie hadn't technically been hidden while at Berk and had in fact attended every event with Hugh, he had felt invisible for all those years, so he wasn't surprised others had perceived him the same way.

Unsure how to respond, he opened and closed his mouth a few times before eventually stammering, "I, uh, hope so." In truth, while he wanted the pride to see him as a person, maybe even as an equal, the only friendship that truly mattered to him was Hugh's.

"Am I wrong about the green beans?" Alexandra asked worriedly.

Johnnie furrowed his brow in confusion.

"You haven't tried them." Alexandra dipped her chin toward the bowl.

"Oh," Johnnie exclaimed. "Right." He wedged the unopened bottle under his arm, picked up the fork, which had been tucked under the food, and scooped up some green beans. "They look wonderful." He took a bite, chewed quickly, and swallowed. "Delicious." The compliment was probably true and Johnnie did love green beans, but at that moment, he couldn't focus on anything other than the shifters he was certain waited outside the festival grounds for a chance to take him and destroy Hugh.

"I'm glad you like them." Alexandra beamed. "I'll make them next time you and Hugh come to a dinner at my pride home." She paused, lowered her gaze to her feet, and hesitantly said. "But I'm not sure where that'll be because, uh, I'm moving."

There was a story there, something she wanted to talk about, and while Johnnie itched to move forward with the plan, he couldn't walk away when she so clearly needed something from him.

"Why are you moving?" he asked.

"Well." She looked up at him and licked her lips. "It's new so I haven't told many people, but I'm pregnant."

"Congratulations," Johnnie said sincerely. "So you're looking at the pride homes for mothers with young cubs?"

She nodded. "I'm narrowing it down right now and then I'll go talk with the heads of a few of them, see if there's room for me." She paused and rubbed her stomach. "For us." She cleared her throat and then whispered, "Can I tell you something?"

"Sure."

Darting her head from side to side, as if to confirm nobody was near them, she stepped closer to Johnnie. "I know things before they happen. Not always, but sometimes. Not *things* but more like ideas." She stopped rambling, shook her head, took a deep breath, and tried again. "I knew we were going to have that big storm last summer even when the sky was clear and blue the day before and lots of times I can tell when our older lions will be called to rest and—" She sighed. "I'm not making sense and everyone always laughs when I say this stuff so you probably think I'm crazy."

"No, I don't." Johnnie shook his head. None of them knew the limitations of their bodies or the gifts they held. His relationship with Hugh was proof of that. "Maybe you have sharper instincts or a closer connection to nature than the rest of us," he suggested.

Her expression brightening, Alexandra said, "I'm glad

you understand. I didn't tell anybody this because they won't believe me, but"—she rubbed her belly again—"I can already feel him."

"You sense you're having a boy?"

"I'm far enough along that the ultrasound shows that." She stepped even closer to Johnnie, their chests brushing. "My baby's a Siphon." She looked up at Johnnie, her face full of excitement. "They'd all think I'm nuts if I said that because there's no test to show it and Siphons are so rare, but I know it." She rubbed both hands over her stomach and smiled down at it happily. "It means I'll have to say goodbye to him when he's barely a man but it also means he's valuable to the pride." She glanced at Johnnie again. "That's good, right? A Siphon is special."

Johnnie reeled from her announcement, not the proclamation that she was carrying a Siphon, because that could be true or not, but rather her reaction to it. Having grown up holed away from danger, people, and life, he hadn't known his mother and had assumed she didn't care enough about him to introduce herself as the woman who bore him, but seeing the joy on Alexandra's face while she talked about her unborn baby, Johnnie wondered if something else had happened. Maybe his mother had passed away when he was too young to remember, as so many lions had in their struggling pride.

"You'll help him, right?" Alexandra asked. "You'll make sure he knows what to do so he can be a useful Siphon?"

What he would do was make sure the cub was included

in the pride instead of ignored. And when the time came for him to connect with a Premier, Johnnie would do anything he could to find him a man as honorable and caring as Hugh.

"I will," Johnnie assured her.

"Thank you!" Alexandra flung her arms around him. The water bottle clunked to the ground and the nearly full bowl of beans upended on his shirt and drizzled onto his pants. "Oh no!" she shouted as she jumped back. "I'm so sorry."

"It's okay." Johnnie picked off the bigger pieces of food and placed them back into the bowl. "I'm sure it'll clean right up." He squatted down, grabbed the bottle, and had an idea. "I'll uh, just go over there." He stood and tilted his chin toward the edge of the festival grounds, where he'd originally been heading. "And I can use this water to wash it off." He held up the bottle.

"It's my fault. I'll do it."

"That's okay. I'll have to undress and I, uh, prefer privacy."

"Oh." Alexandra's brow wrinkled as she pondered that statement. "That's sort of strange, but after what I told you, I shouldn't judge, huh?" She grinned and took the bowl from him. "I'll throw this out and make sure nobody comes out this way, okay? When you're cleaned up, come find me. I made praline pie for dessert and I'll save you a piece."

Johnnie watched Alexandra for a few moments to make sure she didn't decide to turn around and follow him. Once he felt confident she was returning to the eating area, he shook his head to clear it, refocused on his surroundings, and slowly walked toward the edge of the festival grounds. Inhaling deeply, he registered the familiar scents of Berk, the lions who lived there, and the food from that day's meal. He had a flash of a foreign odor, but it was too light to make it out before it disappeared.

He set the water bottle on the ground, slipped out of his jacket, and then ducked his head and began unbuttoning his shirt. In that position, his eyes were hidden from anyone watching, so he took the opportunity to scan the surrounding area. Nothing stood out but the back of his neck prickled telling him something was off. Confident his brain would catch up with his subconscious, he removed his shirt, raised it slightly, and then inhaled deeply, presumably to smell whatever had spilled on it. In actuality, however, he focused on the surrounding areas, not his clothing.

The scent he'd barely caught a hint of earlier was now strong enough to identify. A shifter. Maybe two. Neither of them familiar.

Though Johnnie had anticipated Larry and Dennis bringing reinforcements, he hadn't expected the new additions to come alone. With what he knew about Larry, he doubted the man would give his recruits enough space to double cross him, so if he had sent someone else to grab Johnnie, he had to be waiting for them nearby.

"Crap," he whispered to himself.

Their plan had been for Johnnie to make himself a visible target with Hugh waiting behind rocks nearby but not close enough to be seen or scented. Then, when Larry and company attacked, Hugh would hurry over and they'd disable the intruders. Unfortunately, if they did that, they'd capture the two unknown lions, but Larry and Dennis likely would escape and try again later. Then instead of solving their problem, they'd send the Berk pride a message that their Premier had been thwarted again and they were still in danger. That was an unacceptable outcome and Johnnie internally kicked himself for not having considered this contingency.

He could immediately run over to Hugh and hope the attacking lions would give up for the night, but he had no doubt they'd try again and there was no assurance it'd be at an anticipated time and location. Even worse was the possibility they would become desperate enough to harm a pride member as part of their plot, something that would devastate Hugh and tarnish the pride's confidence in him. No. That wasn't an acceptable choice. They'd have to move forward with their plan, but instead of Hugh jumping in right away, Johnnie would have to let himself be taken and Hugh would need to follow at a distance until they reached Larry and Dennis's waiting spot.

Hoping Hugh would come to the same conclusion, Johnnie quickly shuffled to the right and angled his body so he'd be visible to Hugh if he was peeking from behind the rocks. He then spread his hand in a 'stop' motion in front of his belly, focused all his energy on his connection with Hugh, and mentally sent out a message to wait. Movement sounded in the brush behind him and the strangers' scent got stronger. He lowered his arm, took in a deep breath, and braced himself for an attack.

Wait, Hugh. I'll be okay. Please wait.

Within seconds, the air behind him moved, two arms wrapped around him, and a hand covered his mouth.

"Come quietly and we won't hurt you," said an unfamiliar voice.

That plan meshed well with Johnnie's, but he wriggled a bit and whimpered, putting on a small show so he wouldn't rouse the would-be-kidnappers' suspicions.

"I mean it, Siphon," growled the man as he tightened his grip on Johnnie and shook him.

"Let's go," said the other stranger. He grabbed Johnnie's arm and the two of them dragged him away from the festival grounds and toward the Forest Service land.

Well, at least he'd been right about where Larry and Dennis were hiding. Johnnie stumbled along with the two men, occasionally pretending to struggle and try to escape but not putting on enough of a fight to incite violence because he wanted to be at his strongest when the real battle started.

They'd been walking for fifteen minutes when he first caught Larry's and Dennis's scents.

"We're almost there," said one of the men.

"That was easy," said the other. "Do you think the Premier's already dead or will we have to go farther?"

Red-hot anger burned through Johnnie, but before he could react, they stepped around a thick grouping of trees and shrubs and came face-to-face with Larry.

"You caught him!" he said excitedly. "See, Dennis! I told you it'd work."

Johnnie looked ahead and saw Dennis. He stood quietly, staring in the direction of Berk. His hair was disheveled, his posture slumped, and his expression forlorn.

When Dennis didn't respond, Larry elbowed aside the lion holding Johnnie, dug his fingers into Johnnie's shoulders, and shoved him forward so hard Johnnie lost his balance and fell at Dennis's feet.

"I bet now you're glad you listened to me," Larry said smugly and then looked at the other two men. "Did you have any trouble?"

As Larry and his friends happily chattered about what they'd done and the next step of their plan, Dennis held his hand out for Johnnie and helped him to his feet. "Do you think he's dead?" he asked, his voice cracking and his eyes glistening with unshed tears.

"Why are you doing this?" Johnnie whispered, confused as to why Dennis was involved in something he clearly didn't want.

"I shouldn't have," Dennis said regretfully. He turned his attention back to Berk. "I was stupid and thought I was helping the pride and by the time I realized I wasn't..." He shrugged. "I should have trusted in my Premier. Now it's too late."

"No, it isn't." Johnnie curled his hand around Dennis's forearm, trying to get his attention. "Hugh isn't dead. You can come back to Berk and—"

"I betrayed my pride and my Premier." Dennis swallowed hard. "I can never go back, but"—he searched Johnnie's face—"you're sure he's still alive? Even with you this far apart from him?"

By his estimation, Hugh was no more than a couple of minutes away, but he wasn't going to give away their advantage. "Yes, I'm sure. I'm carrying his power and I can only do that if he's alive."

"The Premier is alive," Dennis whispered. "That means it's not too late."

"It's not," Johnnie agreed. "You can still come back to the pride."

"Dennis, grab the Siphon," Larry said. "We're going to get farther from Berk, just to be sure we're in the clear. Then we can finalize a buyer and—"

"Tell him how sorry I was," Dennis said quietly and then his eyes hardened and he hissed, "Run!"

Other than Hugh, Johnnie had never seen a lion shift as quickly. Before he realized what was happening, Dennis was in his animal form, roaring as he leaped toward Larry.

Confusion, shock, and realization spread over Larry's face in quick succession and then he too began to shift. From his vantage, Johnnie couldn't tell how far Larry had gotten because Dennis was on top of him and, moments later, the other two shifters also took their animal forms and joined the pile. Pained yowls rent the air.

"Dennis!" Johnnie shouted frantically. Even with his unexpected attack and lead-time on the shift, Dennis wouldn't be able to survive a battle against three other lions. Johnnie would have to take his animal form and help him. "I'm coming."

"No, you're not." Hugh's gruff voice rumbled behind Johnnie just before familiar, protective arms tugged him away from the violent scene in front of him and pulled him against a broad chest.

"Hugh." Johnnie nearly sagged in relief. "We have to help Dennis. He won't make it."

"None of them will." Hugh shook his head regretfully as he draped Johnnie's shirt around his back. "I thought you'd be cold so I grabbed this when I followed you." He lifted each of Johnnie's arms and slid them into the sleeves. "I didn't have time to get the green bean stuff off, but at least you'll be warm," he said as he buttoned.

Confused about Hugh's behavior, Johnnie clutched at his chest and said, "Dennis is under those lions. He needs help."

"It's too late." Hugh looked over Johnnie's shoulder at the scene playing out behind him. "A fight that sudden and violent in lion form wrings every ounce of rational thought and adrenaline from us. Their animals have completely taken over. They won't remember who they're battling or why and they won't stop until they're dead."

Almost as quickly as they'd started, the loud screeches ceased, and the scent of blood, thick and heavy, filled the air. Instinctively, Johnnie tried to turn around to see the cause of the change, but Hugh held him close and wouldn't release him.

"You don't want to see this," he said quietly.

"But Dennis was trying to help." Johnnie remembered the despondent expression on Dennis's face as he had gazed toward their pride lands. "He made a mistake and he said he was sorry. He loved Berk."

"Dennis is dead." Hugh glanced at the scene behind Johnnie and then looked at him. "Only one of them is hanging on, but he's on his way out."

A tortured whine came from behind him along with an unnatural gurgling sound.

"We should check." Johnnie tried to turn around again. "He might have made it."

"No." Hugh cupped Johnnie's cheeks. "Listen to me. Their bodies shifted into their human forms and Dennis is—" He cringed. "Dismembered. Larry too. Another one of them had his throat ripped out and the fourth is barely taking in air. They're done. All of them." Hugh hugged Johnnie tightly. "It's over."

CHAPTER 19

As they crossed back into Berk territory, the sounds of adults talking and children laughing greeted them, completely at odds with the horrifying cries and deathly silence still ringing in Johnnie's head.

"Will you be okay here for another little while?" Hugh asked. "I need to take care of the bodies and then we can go home."

The scent of the Thanksgiving meal wafted over and melded with the coppery blood odor Johnnie couldn't clear from his system.

"I'm fine," he answered reflexively.

"You're pale and you're trembling." Hugh stopped walking, tugged on Johnnie's elbow until he faced him, and then he slid his hands over Johnnie's shoulders, massaging him. "I'll take care of you soon, but if we leave their bodies in the open, scavengers will get to them. And Dennis's friends in Berk need to know he died a hero."

Despite the fact that the lions had tried to kill him, Hugh wanted to preserve their dignity in death. And though he had witnessed the same horror as Johnnie, he was concerned about the pride rather than himself. Johnnie gazed at Hugh in admiration.

"I'm okay." Johnnie squared his shoulders. Berk needed its Premier and the Premier needed his Siphon. "What should we do?"

Smiling softly at him, Hugh curled his palms around Johnnie's neck and brushed his thumbs against the sensitive skin behind Johnnie's ears. "You're wonderful." He hunched down, and pressed his lips to Johnnie's. "I love you."

Johnnie ran his hands over Hugh's chest, the heat and strength arousing and reassuring. "I love you too."

"Let's find Van Hartwick. He can gather some of the lions from his den to bury the dead. I don't want Percy or the others who lived with Dennis to see his remains."

Nodding in agreement, Johnnie followed Hugh to the center of the gathering. Years of experience helped him appear fine despite his uneasy stomach and frayed nerves. He disappeared into the background easily, remaining close to Hugh but out of the way, present but unobtrusive. Now that he accepted his role, Johnnie fell into it without resentment or hesitation.

His pace unhurried, Hugh walked by various pride members, nodding in greeting and answering a few questions. Most people likely would have considered his demeanor calm as usual but Johnnie saw the slight stiffness in his shoulders, the tick in his jaw, and the way he pressed his fingers into the base of his skull, as if to push away tension.

"Van," Hugh said when they finally reached the area where Van Hartwick stood talking with a group of shifters.

"Did you enjoy the meal?"

"Yes, Premier. Thank you for planning this."

"Good." Hugh reached his hand out, and when Van took it, clapped Van on the shoulder, leaned close, and said, "Come talk to me." With Van on his tail, Hugh turned around and stepped away from the others.

Johnnie kept his distance, giving them privacy.

They talked for a few minutes, Hugh shook Van's hand, and then Van walked toward the center of the gathering, darting his gaze around, presumably to locate the lions he'd take with him.

"How did it go?" Johnnie asked Hugh when he approached.

"Van is a good man. He'll take care of the bodies." Hugh sighed and rubbed his palms over his eyes. "Now I need to talk to Percy and a few others who were close to Dennis individually, and then I'll update the pride as a whole."

Thoughtful, systematic, thorough. "You're a wonderful Premier and this pride is lucky to have you." Johnnie cleared his throat. "I'm lucky to have you."

"I feel the same way about them." Hugh gazed at him warmly. "And you."

"What are you thinking about so hard that it's keeping you from sleeping?" Hugh asked as he pressed his lips to the top of Johnnie's head and caressed his back.

Johnnie lay partially on top of Hugh, his face pillowed on Hugh's chest, his groin pressed against Hugh's hip, and his left leg tucked between both of Hugh's.

"How could you tell I wasn't sleeping?"

"You breathe differently when you're asleep." Hugh ran his hand over the curve of Johnnie's ass.

"I like how you know that about me." Johnnie turned his head slightly and kissed Hugh's nipple.

"Me too."

He flicked his tongue out, swirled it over Hugh's nipple, and suckled him for a few moments. "I was thinking about what Dennis did."

"Uh-huh," Hugh said encouragingly.

"It was the complete opposite of what game theory would have predicted."

"Why's that?"

"Well." Johnnie gathered his thoughts. "In game theory, if people stick together, the group as a whole benefits more, but if a person looks out only for himself, he's better off individually. If Dennis was worried about being caught, he could have run off and left Larry and the others there to take the fall. That would have benefited him individually but hurt the group. Or if he wanted to help the group above himself, he could have worked with Larry and the other two shifters and taken me farther from you faster so they wouldn't get caught. They had no idea how close you were so in his mind that approach would have worked. But he didn't do either of those things."

"He attacked Larry instead," Hugh said.

"Yes." Johnnie dipped his chin. "And he knew it was a death sentence. I didn't notice at the time because everything happened so fast, but I was thinking back to that moment and I remember him asking me to tell you how sorry he was." Johnnie laid his forearm across Hugh's chest and propped his chin on it so he could meet Hugh's gaze. "He said *'was.'* Like he knew he'd be dead by the time I told you."

"He probably did. His latest actions aside, Dennis wasn't dumb. He also wasn't selfish. And what he did followed the game theory concept, just in a more extreme way."

"What do you mean?" Johnnie asked, scrunching his eyebrows together.

"The theory is that if an individual works for the group instead of himself, he won't be as well off but the group will benefit more as a whole, right?"

"Yes. But Dennis attacked the group. He wasn't trying to make them better off."

"You're thinking of the wrong group." Hugh traced Johnnie's eyebrows with his fingertip. "At the end of the day, Dennis's loyalty lay with Berk. This pride was his group and he was willing to sacrifice his own life for the well-being of his pridemates."

"That makes sense." Johnnie nodded in understanding. "It's why you said he died a hero."

"Right. He made mistakes so profound, I couldn't see him as anything other than a traitor and an enemy. But then he put the pride's well-being above his own and showed his trust in me as the Premier in the most fundamental way possible." Hugh curled his huge palm around Johnnie's head and pulled him forward for a kiss. "Plus, he died trying to save you. That makes him a hero in my book."

While that was technically true, Dennis's ultimate reason for trying to help Johnnie escape had been to save Hugh's life, not Johnnie's. But the distinction didn't matter. The bottom line was that Dennis gave the ultimate sacrifice for Berk's good.

The depth of Dennis's devotion put Johnnie's upbringing into perspective. He now understood why his birth pride had never considered a life for him outside of being a Siphon—the pride would whither without a Premier and he alone held the ability to keep the Premier alive. And having experienced firsthand the violent actions of shifters who wanted to possess him for their own greedy purposes, Johnnie now recognized the wisdom in keeping a Siphon secure and protected.

"Were you close enough to overhear my conversation with Alexandra?" Johnnie asked.

"A few words here and there. Not enough to understand anything. Why? What did she say?"

"She's pregnant and she thinks her baby is a Siphon."

"Really?" Hugh arched his eyebrows. "What gives her that impression?"

Shrugging, Johnnie said, "She senses it."

"Well, putting aside whether it's possible to sense the

nature of an unborn cub, something like one of every half million lions is born a Siphon. Having two in the same pride seems like a long shot."

"Probably," Johnnie agreed. "But let's say she's right. Let's say that within the year, we have another Siphon in Berk. A tiny, defenseless Siphon." Johnnie sat up, crossed his legs, and dragged his fingers through his hair. "I spent my childhood depressed and resentful about being excluded from everyone, but when I think about that baby and what the Larrys of the world could do to him, I want to build a tower, surround it with an alligator-filled moat, and lock the cub at the very top."

"That's a very vivid and very...old-fashioned image." Hugh chuckled. "One thing you need to remember is that you were born into a small, dying pride. The Westgate lions struggled to keep themselves alive. They didn't have the resources to protect you in any way other than keeping you locked up. We're a Premier Pride. If we're blessed with a Siphon being born in Berk, we have the resources to both protect and nurture him."

Johnnie sighed in relief.

His expression turning serious, Hugh sat up. "The other thing Berk has is a Premier who learns from his mistakes." He took Johnnie's hand between his. "I made the worst mistakes of my life with you and it nearly killed us both." He ran his palms over Johnnie's chest, across his shoulders, and wrapped them around both sides of his neck. "As it is, my blindness cost us years apart even when we were in the same room." He tipped his forehead forward and leaned it against Johnnie's. "If our pride has a young Siphon, we will not be selling him to the highest bidder. He will have a home here for as long as he wants it. Nobody will own him."

Articulating the lesson he learned from Dennis's sacrifice, Johnnie said, "It'd be wrong to leave a pride to languish by withholding a Siphon from a Premier who would die without him. Prides need their Premier and a Siphon has to fulfill his role."

"That's true." Hugh slid his thumbs across Johnnie's cheekbones and massaged his fingertips over the back of Johnnie's head. "How about we teach him how important he is, how necessary, and then we let him choose a pride and a Premier he wants to spend his life with?"

"That's a good plan."

"Do you know how important you are to me, Johnnie?" Hugh lowered Johnnie onto his back and then lay over him. "I adore you." He ran the tip of his tongue around the perimeter of Johnnie's lips. "I need you." He shuddered and his voice grew hoarse with emotion. "I cherish you."

"You have me," Johnnie promised. "I understand my place in the pride now, the importance of my role. And I always wanted you but now..." He gulped, his throat suddenly thick and rough. "You fill me completely. My head, my heart, my soul." Desire sharp in its intensity struck Johnnie. "Please." He trembled. "I need you." He wrapped his legs around Hugh's waist and tilted his backside up, opening himself to be filled in a more primal way.

"I love you." Hugh smiled at him, the corners of his eyes crinkling, his expression affectionate and serene. "I'm glad I can show you like this." He blindly reached for the bottle of lubricant on the nightstand and made quick work of getting them both ready. "But if I get so busy with the pride that I forget to show you in other ways, tell me." He slanted his mouth over Johnnie's and kissed him tenderly as he pressed the wide, smooth head of his erection against Johnnie's puckered opening. "I promise to always listen to you." Slowly, Hugh slid into him.

"You're their Premier," Johnnie said breathlessly, his back bowing as he took the thick heat all the way inside him. "They need you."

Hugh nuzzled Johnnie's neck. "They need their Premier. I need my Siphon." He slowly pulled out and then rocked back in. "It all goes together."

Spines grew on Hugh's cock, massaging each of Johnnie's nerve endings as he pumped in and out of his passage. Clawing at Hugh's back, Johnnie gasped, and said, "*We* go together."

They moved in unison, bodies, minds, and hearts connecting as they gave and sought fulfillment and release. Hugh mouthed Johnnie's lips, nibbled on his earlobes, and sucked on his neck. He grazed his hands over whatever parts of Johnnie he could reach, like he couldn't get enough.

Johnnie felt the same way. "I was meant for this," he whispered.

"You were meant for me."

Deep in his soul, where he had once been cold, empty, and lonely and he was now warm, fulfilled, and loved, Johnnie knew that was true.

"Your Siphon," he said as he fell over the edge of pleasure into blinding bliss, seed pulsing from his cock.

"My Johnnie." Hugh ground his hips against him, moaned, and then kissed him deeply as he came. "Mine."

THE END

REVIEWS

Jumping In: Loved, Loved, Loved this book! It was the perfect Valentine's week read and hit all my squishy feelings.

— *Guilty Indulgence*

Blue Mountain: Blue Mountain had plenty of character interaction along with the perfect blend of heart tugging moments, passion and humor.

— *Swept Away by Romance*

In Another Life & Eight Days: I love Cardeno C. novellas. They are short, sweet, hot, poignant and pack a punch. Perfect writing, brilliant characters and hilarious banter.

— *Two Book Pushers*

Just What the Truth Is: This was a wonderful story and the chemistry was off the charts.

— *Wicked Reads*

Where He Ends and I Begin: It is also sexy and smutty, and filled with a very large amount of dirty fun.

— *Prism Book Alliance*

He Completes Me: The piece was well written, entertaining, and emotional – a total win for me.

— *Redz World*

ABOUT THE AUTHOR

Cardeno C.—CC to friends—is a hopeless romantic who wants to add a lot of happiness and a few *awwws* into a reader's day. Writing is a nice break from real life as a corporate type and volunteer work with gay rights organizations. Cardeno's stories range from sweet to intense, contemporary to paranormal, long to short, but they always include strong relationships and walks into the happily-ever-after sunset.

Email: cardenoc@gmail.com

Website: www.cardenoc.com

Twitter: https://twitter.com/cardenoc

Facebook: http://www.facebook.com/CardenoC

Pinterest: http://www.pinterest.com/cardenoC

Blog: http://caferisque.blogspot.com

OTHER BOOKS BY CARDENO C.

AVAILABLE NOW

Blue Mountain

(A Pack Story)

Exiled by his pack as a teen, Omega wolf Simon Moorehead learns to bury his gentle nature in the interest of survival. When a hulking, rough-faced Alpha catches Simon on pack territory, he tries to escape what he's sure will be imminent death. But instead of killing him, the Alpha takes Simon home.

A man of action, Mitch Grant uproots his life to support his brother in leading the Blue Mountain pack. Mitch lives on the periphery, quietly protecting everyone, but always alone. A mate is a dream come true for Mitch, and he won't let little things like Simon's rejections, attacks, and insults get in their way. With patience, seduction, and genuine care, Mitch will ride out the storm while Simon slays his own ghosts and Mitch's loneliness.

McFarland's Farm

(A Hope Story)

Wealthy, attractive Lucas Reika treats life like a party, moving from bar to bar and man to man. Thumbing his nose at his restaurateur father's demand that he earn his keep, Lucas instead seduces a valued employee in the kitchen of their flagship restaurant, earning himself an ultimatum: lose access to his father's money or stay in the middle of nowhere with a man he has secretly lusted over from afar.

Quiet, hard-working Jared McFarland loves his farm on the outskirts of Hope, Arizona, but he aches to have someone to come home to at the end of the day. Jared agrees to take in his longtime crush as a favor. But when Lucas invades his heart in addition to his space, Jared has to decide how much of himself he's willing to risk and figure out if he can offer Lucas enough to keep him after his father's punishment is over.

In Another Life

At age eighteen, Shiloh Raben is tired. He no longer has the energy to deal with mean classmates, inner doubt, and fear of familial rejection, so he takes a razor to his wrist. When he wakes up in the hospital, Shiloh meets Travis Kahn, the EMT who saved him and didn't leave his side.

Travis is handsome, smart, and funny—the type of guy Shiloh would never be brave enough to approach. But his near-death experience has an unusual side effect: the life that flashed before his eyes wasn't the one he had already lived, but rather the one he could live. With visions of a future by Travis's side, Shiloh will find the strength to confront his fears and build a life worth fighting for.

Eight Days

Childhood family friends, Maccabe Fried and Josh Segal have always gotten along despite having nothing in common. Maccabe is an athlete with dreams of playing professional baseball. Josh is an aspiring architect with dreams of being with Maccabe. Despite all odds, both dreams come true.

Maccabe and Josh fall into a long-distance romance, which is everything Josh thought he wanted. But after years of hiding from the world, Josh wants to bring their relationship into the open. When Maccabe refuses, Josh is faced with a tough decision: stay with the man he loves or live the life he deserves. No matter the choice, somebody's bound to get hurt. Thankfully, in the season of miracles, there's always hope for a happy ending.

Walk With Me

(A Home Story)

When Eli Block steps into his parents' living room and sees his childhood crush sitting on the couch, he starts a shameless campaign to seduce the young rabbi. Unfortunately, Seth Cohen barely remembers Eli and he resolutely shuts down all his advances. As a tenuous and then binding friendship forms between the two men, Eli must find a way to move past his unrequited love while still keeping his best friend in his life. Not an easy feat when the same person occupies both roles.

Professional, proper Seth is shocked by Eli's brashness, overt sexuality, and easy defiance of societal norms. But he's also drawn to the happy, funny, light-filled man. As their friendship deepens over the years, Seth watches Eli mature into a man he admires and respects. When Seth finds himself longing for what Eli had so easily offered, he has to decide whether he's willing to veer from his safe life-plan to build a future with Eli.

www.ingramcontent.com/pod-product-compliance
Lightning Source LLC
Chambersburg PA
CBHW060422180626
46817CB00007B/2619